CAPTAIN CARDINAL
and the Crimson Crest

Clayton Varney

ISBN: 978-1-962231-45-9(Hardback)
ISBN: 978-1-962231-44-2 (Paperback)
ISBN: 978-1-962231-46-6 (Ebook)

Published by: Crosswords Noble House
Cover Design by: Crosswords Noble House
Interior Design by: Crosswords Noble House

Book Ordering Information:

Crosswords Noble House
165 Broadway Suite 23rd Floor,
New York, NY 10006, USA

info@crosswordsnoblehouse.com
www.crosswords noblehouse.com
(667) 910-8318 | Ext. 101

Printed in the United States of America

ACKNOWLEDGEMENTS

This book has been a long time in the making and faced many challenges, myself being the biggest one. Thank you for sticking it out, Clayton.

Glory goes to the Infinite Spirit and the Lord Christ within me, for illuminating the gift of imagination, and brilliantly teaching me the beloved to write in many ways through the process of writing this fantastic story. Having these wonderful characters to play with and letting them decide their own fate was such a joy.

Thank you also to my mom. You have always loved me and supported my creative spirit. I love you. My dad's spirit is in heaven. He was an outstanding trumpet player, to say the least, and I credit him also for the part he played in my manifold creativity. Thanks to my brothers, Jacob and David. You have always been in my life, pretty darn close for most of it, and we've all got a lot to be thankful for. Thank you both also for helping edit and proofread this manuscript. Thank you also to everyone else who has been and is part of this journey with me.

CHAPTER I: DREAMING

Dear adventurer, let me first apologize. Over a decade ago, another version of this story was recorded by a rather impetuous storyteller who, to his own admission, left out quite a bit and got a lot of the rest wrong. Feeling a more accurate portrayal of this epic hero demanded my devoted attention, I have spent nearly a decade researching what really happened, making use of the captain's log, his own private journal, and what those involved had to say of their fantastic experiences with the legendary Captain Cardinal of Animystia. Unfortunately, I have to say that this work was even stolen and printed before it could be completed, but the reader may trust this volume to be the definitive rendition of this narrative.

The story of Captain Cardinal begins on Earth, with the Tellurian called Jack Diamond, on a night that would alter both his own destiny and that of an unearthly realm. As a Tellurian, he had a thriving business as an exceptional carpenter, a wife he genuinely loved to the extent of his ability, and some other very enjoyable relationships. He seemed really quite satisfied with the way his life was progressing, but he was yet unaware that Earth is a world of image and illusion, and in the deepest recesses of his heart, there existed a longing for transformation. He was thirty years old that night when the visitors from Animystia arrived, with whom he left.

As it happens, Jack had always had a rampant imagination, and it was nothing strange for him to have dreams of a rather vibrant sort. On this particular night, they had their usual ethereal quality, though they were bolstered with a new seemingly tangible reality. Impressed, he gazed upon the brilliant images mysteriously staking their claim on the morphing plane of his imagination.

The tragic scene opened on the cusp of a great betrayal. Jack found himself looking intently into a great hall enclosed within a cylindrical stone wall. At its center was a round wooden table, decorated with a blazoned phoenix crest. Encircling it were twelve golden thrones, three of which were unoccupied. Two were supposed to be empty, but tensions were mounting over the vacancy of the third. A regal pair sat in thrones with higher backs, distinguishing them as king and queen, and their son was to the king's right.

What had distinctly impressed Jack regarding the assembled coterie was their unusual nature. In form and appearance, all of them were like Tellurian men and women, yet with obvious birdlike attributes such as beaks and feathered wings. The queen's feathers were white as snow, and the king's head and tail feathers matched his bride's, though the rest of his plumage was a compelling dark brown.

Jack watched as the king suddenly stood and gazed intently above him through the skylight entryway. The latter noticed his betrayer, accompanied by five others, about to break in. The brutal grey-and-plum-clad figure had a terrifying weapon in his hand, and it was pointed at the king; Jack recognized it as a handcannon, but the assembly seemed to be thrown off by it. With a flash, the sound of a fired round penetrating the glass preceded a frightening injury to the king.

One of the two non-Avian adversaries was a black-and-yellow Vespan with a deadly stinger, who proceeded to shatter the bullet-cracked glass with a menacing spear, allowing the villainous party an entrance. The other had apple-green skin and spiny projections, like a poisonous caterpillar, one from each of her shoulder-blades and one from just above each of her buttocks. While the others had wings, she descended using a grappling hook attached to a device on her wrist.

"Mockingbird!" a chorus of surprised and terrified nobles exclaimed.

The ringleader touched down on the table in front of the royal pair and sharply demanded, "King Eagle, surrender the crown! Your mockery of a reign is at an end." He cocked the weapon and aimed it at the king again, who had collapsed back into his throne. The latter's hand was over part of his face, blood dripping through his fingers.

When Mockingbird's accomplices began to engage, the prince commanded, "Lords, seize them!"

The four Avian lords had already stood from their thrones and drawn their swords. One of the two largest was directly behind Mockingbird and, spreading his enormous brown-and-white wings in a terrifyingly magnificent way, began to lunge. The insurrectionist pivoted and pulled the trigger, then turned back to the king, the body of Sir Osprey bleeding out on the table behind him.

At a loss, as Mockingbird clearly had the upper hand (for they had not but swords to defend against the ranged terror of a firearm), the king attempted to reason with his betrayer. "Lord Mockingbird, what have you done? Sir Osprey took up your appointment after you forfeited it. You were both like brothers at this table, at our table."

"Brother?" Lord Mockingbird spat derisively. "You always claimed equality, but we were never equal. I guess anyone can fill a seat at your table though. You certainly had no problem replacing me with..." he looked back with disdain at Sir Osprey, "this?" Resuming his stance, he went on, "Furthermore, Lord Mockingbird is disgraceful. Call me Major Mockingbird now. I am your major failure and your major downfall."

The scene shifted, and Jack found himself peering into the king's solar, where the injured, broken, and weeping ruler had been helped to escape Mockingbird by two of the lords. They were standing guard while he prayed. He was staggering over ancient-looking pages of sacred writings that were scattered about on the bloodied floor beneath him. With one of the tattered pages in his feeble grip, he cried out the name "Phoenix Prime!" pleading, "Let the prophecy of Captain Cardinal be fulfilled!"

Suddenly, there came the sound of a mighty rushing wind, and the castle shook around them. On high alert, the two lords dashed into the room to investigate, but they were immobilized in wonder. Along with the king, they marveled as they beheld a bright crimson flame embolden the stained-glass window encased in the northern face of the cylindrical solar wall, which told of many things concerning Captain Cardinal. Awe further struck each of them as the bird of his namesake sprang forth as a tiny winged incarnation.

The little red avian creature alighted on the floor in front of the king and began to speak to him beneficently. "Fear not, King Eagle, I am Carnelian. Phoenix Prime has heard you, and your prayer is answered. I have come as an emissary to bring to you the one you need." While the king wept with tears of relief and thankfulness toward Phoenix Prime, Carnelian commissioned him, "Have Sir Albatross and Lord Peacock ready the Crimson Crest. They must accompany me, and I will guide them."

"I understand," the king replied, full of hope.

"We understand," they echoed.

"King Eagle," Carnelian exhorted, "pray for the one to whom we go, for he must make the choice to come back with us, or all hope is lost."

The dreamscape shifted again, and Jack was surrounded by clouds illuminated by crimson moonlight. Planks of glistening red wood and a tall mast of the same, along with a billowing crimson sail, revealed an airborne ship. Two animated silhouettes of distinctly different sizes were conversing about him at the helm. A third much smaller silhouette flitted into view, perched on the wheel, and chirped in a way Jack had never heard cardinals do before. He heard the name "Rainbow Veil," and a swirling mass of every color imaginable (and even colors yet to be imagined) suddenly appeared. Just as the portal closed neatly around the rear of the ship, Jack woke up.

Chapter II: The Impossible Choice

Upon his abrupt return to consciousness, Jack was initially perplexed regarding his whereabouts. As his eyes adjusted to the eerie pinkish moonlight spilling in through his window, he realized he had fallen asleep at the desk in his private study. Yawning and feeling more at ease, he stretched himself out over his velvet armchair. He glanced at the old-fashioned desk clock with the cardinal motif in front of him; it showed the time to be 2:42 AM.

Rather that returning to sleep, he sat cross-legged in silence, contemplating that which he had just dreamed and its inherent meaning. While doing so, he noticed how the rosy light being cast across his cherry-wood desk enriched its color, and he remembered the blood moon in the December forecast. He wondered affectionately if his wife, who was away, was enjoying the phenomenon from her current vantage point.

As he thought to open the window for a better view himself, he saw a swooping
shadow and heard a faint tapping sound on the glass. Completely forgetting the lunar spectacle, he carefully lifted the window frame, but the source of the distraction had gone. He remained alert and waited, not knowing what to expect.

Frustration began to set in until his eyes met the old cherry tree, whose snowy branches might have clawed at the frosted window if the icy wind had persuaded them. He laughed and remembered the scarlet sky, taking it in before a tiny chortle echoed. Distracted again, he let his eyes descend to see a crimson bird not at all unlike the one he had just dreamed about. It perched conspicuously on the windowsill, peering up at him with eyes like flames of fire, igniting his imagination.

"Hello, Jack, I am Carnelian," the creature formally introduced itself.

The Tellurian suddenly realized his recent vision may not have been a dream after all. This conclusion demanded an explanation, and he was about to do just that when Carnelian leaped to his right shoulder and sharply bit his earlobe. Yelping in shock and disbelief, he clapped the wound with his palm to pressurize it. He swiped at and missed Carnelian with the other hand. It had been merely a peck, and he quickly determined the bleeding to be negligible, but was still very much annoyed. He attempted to retaliate, but the bird-form darted back through the window and retreated into the darkness from whence it came, robbing him of the chance.

Placing his hands on his desk, Jack stuck his head out the window in search of the elusive enigma, whereupon he saw something else that conflicted with his current perception of reality. "There's no way," he whispered, as he beheld an enormous object suspended in the moonlit sky, nearly indistinguishable in color from its circular backdrop. The mast and sails he had seen in his dream gained context as he began to realize that what he beheld indeed was a ship, constructed primarily of wood of a crimson hue unlike any on Earth and a vibrant reddish metal that was similarly unfamiliar.

The question of whatever mechanics allowed the vessel to remain airborne perplexed and intrigued him. He made a few hypotheses based on external observation and logic, and fancied being able to investigate the technology's real secret at an opportune time. More pressing than the subject of his study was the implication of what was presently happening on his account. Continuing to survey the vessel as it descended, he marveled at the sight of the pair at the helm, whom he supposed to be the two with whom Carnelian had requested to make the journey, Sir Albatross and Lord Peacock.

"Ahoy there," he heard one of them hail in a high tone he guessed must have come from Lord Peacock.

Fortunately, Jack lived on a rather large estate, and he had no neighbors to speak of who were near enough to have either witnessed any of this otherworldly spectacle or been within earshot of the colloquial greeting.

"Are you Lord Peacock and Sir Albatross?" Jack inquired.

"Yes, we are! Come on!" they shouted back.

Needing answers to a multitude of questions, Jack hastily mostly closed the window and left the room, neglecting at all to close the door behind him. He dashed down the stairs and bolted through the front doorway just as the ship stabilized, the spectacular anti-gravitational engineering allowing the vessel to remain suspended just above the ground without any physical support. Entranced and dumbfounded by this apparent manifestation of his subconscious, he continued staring with wide eyes while the emphatic efforts of encouragement from the two aboard the ship washed over him.

A newly familiar chirp snapped him out his trance. "Come one, Jack, we have to go," Carnelian observed, and darted toward the helm of the ship.

After a brief hesitation, with the urgent voices of Sir Albatross and Lord Peacock now ringing in his ears, Jack began to consider the necessity of getting aboard the ship. As he did so, a hinged compartment in the side of it began to unfold downward, revealing a built-in staircase. Gaining resolve, he made his way toward the steps that would mark the beginning of a wondrous path on which his wildest fantasies had never dared to tread. The moment his foot touched the first, he knew there was no turning back. Despite thoughts of his wife and business trying desperately to make him do so, he was unable to ignore the overwhelming adventure that was calling him by name, and he pressed on against all reason to stay.

As he neared the open hatch, a large hand in a black leather glove was offered to him, and he grabbed it. Bringing him to the ship's deck was Sir Albatross, who was a giant in Jack's eyes. The hulking Avian lord stood over seven feet tall, according to Jack's estimation, and he possessed exceptionally broad shoulders. Unfolded and extended, his wings (which were mostly shadow grey) were also quite impressive, but Jack would have to wait to see their full span. The rest of his feathers were white as snow, and his pinkish beak was long and narrow, the upper mandible curving down over the lower.

Upon having taken inventory of Sir Albatross' appearance, Jack fixed his attention on the Avian's much smaller counterpart, Lord Peacock. He was thinner by far, and at least a foot shorter, but still muscular. He wore dark teal pants and a rust-colored vest, with matching boots and gloves. The attire complimented his striking blue coat and stunning array of brilliantly-colored tail feathers. Sir Albatross released his grasp, and Jack offered his hand in turn to Lord Peacock.

Carnelian, still settled on the shining ruby-laden helm, chirped again to gain their collective attention. When Jack laid eyes on him again, indignity resurfaced as he tenderly felt his earlobe where it had been bitten without warning or explanation. Adopting an angry spirit, he moved to swing at the wee bird, but Sir Albatross extended his enormous arm across Jack's chest to hold him back.

"Jack, give Carnelian a chance to explain," he said with a cool temper.

Coming to his senses, Jack apologized and bade the avian creature to do so.

"Thank you, Jack Diamond," Carnelian said. "I do apologize. I know this is all very sudden for you, and there is much you will learn in time, but it wouldn't do to tell you everything now. Concerning you ear, I meant no ill will. I simply needed your blood for the transformation."

"What transformation?" Jack demanded.

"The one that will occur if you choose to journey on with us into your destiny."

"My destiny?"

"Yes. You are Jack Diamond, a Tellurian, are you not?"

"I am Jack Diamond. What's a Tellurian?"

"This is Earth, is it not?"

"Uhh, yes."

"The blood of your people is, shall we say, special. You, Jack, are very special."

Jack couldn't help but laugh at the absurdity of what he'd just heard, but he was apparently the only one present who thought it was so. He scanned the faces of both lords and, finding them inscrutable, returned his attention to Carnelian. "Look," he said, "you'll have to forgive me if this is all a little lost on me."

"I know, Jack," the bird acknowledged. "This is an impossible choice for you. You may come with us, have your questions answered, and find out your true intended destiny. Otherwise, you may depart back to your house, try and forget about all this, and go on with your life as you've known it."

A spirit of fear immediately seized Jack. The excuses concerning his wife, business, and whole life on Earth that he'd bypassed earlier began to get in his way. He looked desperately at the two lords, hoping to get some sort of sympathy, but none was given.

Lowering his beak patiently, Carnelian gave Jack a moment to wrestle with the decision. Afterward, the incarnation fixed his fiery gaze on the Tellurian once again and said with great compassion, "It is true that you will have to make sacrifices if you come with us, and I know the difficulty you face in not knowing what lies ahead if you choose to make them. You can only have faith that what you gain will be greater than what you are leaving behind."

Sir Albatross took a step forward and added with the utmost sincerity, "There are things we've had that we could never have imagined living without. In light of the friends and family we've lost, many of those things seem insignificant now."

Jack nearly shot an indignant glance at Sir Albatross with the notion, "What do you know?" However, he felt the gentle giant's pain, and the angry thought was dispelled. Shaking his head, he sighed, "This is an impossible choice."

With a final word of exhortation, Lord Peacock added, "Jack, you must come of your own free will. If your life here in this world is exactly as you desire, then stay and live it to the fullest. If upon searching your heart, however, you find a longing there for something more, something you know this world cannot provide, then what choice do you really have?"

Jack enjoyed the pleasures of his life on Earth to a somewhat enviable level, but he had begun to realize he couldn't keep living for what was merely himself any longer. He knew this was about something much bigger. As the trio waited patiently for an answer, he looked up and queried curiously, "So, where are we going?"

Delighted, Carnelian bowed to show his eternal gratitude. "Animystia," he replied, and swept a wing in the direction of the spectacular sight that spiraled in the atmosphere before them.

"Whoa!" Jack wondered aloud at the swirling mass of ethereal color, that had also made its debut in his prophetic dream, woven into the velvet blanket of the night.

"That is the Rainbow Veil," Carnelian answered. "It's our way home."

Chapter III: A Veiled Threat

Sir Albatross' demeanor, which had been cheerful on account of Jack's decision to come back with them, suddenly changed. He arched his head in full alert, directing his attention to the strangely illumined void, monitoring it intently. A subtle gleam of light reflecting from something just inside confirmed his suspicion and, taking his cue, the party braced for the impending ambush. His gut told him that the glint he had perceived was from the silver blade of a certain former compatriot, and was proven right when the dark blur emerged, speeding with the velocity of an arrow straight toward him.

"Get down!" he shouted, and he drew his sword, pivoting just in time to avoid decapitation. Metal struck metal, and the force of impact launched his cutlass from his grasp and knocked him to the ship's deck. A favorite memory of a long-ago sparring match flashed in his mind, and his spirit quickened. Summoning his strength, he began to raise himself up.

His adversary picked up his sword and stood over him, gloating. A black head, contrasted with white under his beak and down his front, gave him the appearance of an executioner. Adding to the effect, he wore dark garb with razor-sharp talon-like silver armor plating, which ominously reflected the moon's haunting glare.

"Uunghh, Lord Peregrine," Sir Albatross acknowledged, emphasizing the title his fallen compatriot had renounced, "I knew it was you. Who else could move so fast?"

Acknowledging the sincerity of the compliment, Peregrine answered, "Sir Albatross, even with me as your enemy, you are too kind."
A mutual respect passed between them, and Peregrine allowed Sir Albatross to his feet, though they both knew what was about to occur.

"I am sorry it had to come to this, old friend," he offered with sincerity, tossing Albatross his weapon. "You had become my strength."

The ever-ready swashbuckler deftly caught his weapon by the hilt and, pointing the blade in a friendly gesture toward his foe, returned the sentiment, "Yes, comrade, and you had become my speed. I'm sorry you chose to leave us, but I know you always thought King Eagle was foolish for believing in the prophecy. You never did."

"That's right," Peregrine confirmed, "I do not believe in the prophecy or anyone that has hope in it."

"Still, you would rather join Mockingbird's rebellion?"

"What choice did I have?"

"You always have a choice, my friend. I pray that, should you survive this, you learn to make your own."

"Duly noted," his former ally assented. "Shall we?"

"If it has to be," the honorable lord lamented.
While they each held their swords aloft, squaring off for their inevitable duel, another shadowy form appeared

out of the chromatic vortex, making a beeline straight for Jack. As it approached, Lord Peacock prepared to intercept it, only to be dismayed when what had appeared to be one threat became two; they had both flown in on a compact aerial vessel, and one had dismounted via his own means of flight. They were the two non-Avians in Jack's dream.

Lord Peacock could often be somewhat overconfident, but he wasn't foolish enough to think he would be able to take on both of them at the same time, and with Sir Albatross already mortally engaged, his options were severely limited. "Jack!" he shouted. "Can you fight?"

"I can!" the Tellurian shouted back. As it turns out, Jack had actually studied fencing in school, and he was pretty handy with a sword.

"Get below, and find the armaments! I'll try and hold them off!" Favor was with Lord Peacock, for though he was momentarily distracted, the tiny poisonous dart that was meant for his unguarded neck narrowly missed its target. The petite projectile simply passed through an iridescent eye spot embellishing his ornate plumage and found itself embedded in the wooden deck of the ship instead. The device on the pilot's wrist also acted as a miniature crossbow, and her accuracy was usually unfailing, so her errant shot angered her tremendously.

She hastily reloaded and fired another dart in frustration, but Lord Peacock was on his guard this time. His rapier flashed with a clink, and the minute missile ricocheted back at her. Relief at also having barely avoided it herself was suddenly replaced by panic as she realized the wind turbine of her aircraft was no longer spinning, and she'd lost control.

In her descent, she instinctively leaped from her defunct vehicle and found herself clinging to the mast of the Crimson Crest. Her ally was speedily buzzing toward Lord Peacock as well, but was forced to slow his advance when she nearly collided with him. She also managed to damage her weapon, which further served to give Peacock the advantage.

- - -

Below, meanwhile, the weaponry had taken relatively little time to for Jack to locate. He'd spotted a red wooden chest with a black metallic latch and set himself to open it. Thinking on acquiring a sword from within, he wasn't quite prepared for what he found clinging inside its lid.

Startled, he flung the chest open, jolting the sleeping occupant awake. An amphibious green-skinned stowaway leaped to the wall and clung to it. Mouth agape, Jack marveled at the voluminous pale golden eyes staring down at him and the figure's dangling blonde mohawk. She was confused and frightened, but his presence quickened her, and she formed a wide smile.

The sounds of battle overhead immediately brought to both of them the urgency to join it. Introducing herself to Jack as Hyla, the stowaway whipped her elastic tongue into the chest and fetched a small sword, putting it within his reach. Impressed, he took ahold of it. His new ally proceeded to reveal her own weapon from a clasp on the back of her belt, a six-inch cylindrical device with a sharp spike on either end.

Upon emerging from the hatch, Jack immediately noticed Peregrine and Sir Albatross undertaken with their duel. Saddleback (the one on the mast) was at the same time watching as Yellowjacket (the one with the spear) was heading toward Lord Peacock again. The Tellurian then noticed Saddleback, who noticed him at the same time, but they were too far away from each other for a melee, and she was angered yet again by her ranged weapon being out of commission.

As Hyla came out from behind Jack, she quickly discerned her role and leaped toward the mast, beginning to climb. Saddleback instinctively grabbed a rope within reach and swung around to elude her dexterous pursuer. Hyla reached behind her, retrieved her spiked weapon, and tossed it into the air. A fraction of a second later, her adhesive whip-like tongue was secured to its center, and was aiming for an apple-green thigh. Saddleback, in another reflexive maneuver, barely managed to avoid getting impaled and plummeting either to the deck below or overboard. Feeling the thrill of a challenge, Hyla retracted her tongue and smiled, the deadly instrument resting between her wide lips, its points protruding from either side.

"Yellowjacket!" Saddleback cried. "Get up here!"

Yellowjacket's attention became divided, and the distraction gave Lord Peacock the opening he needed. In an instant, the latter's blade neatly sliced his opponent's head off at the neck, and it rolled comically. Saddleback's distressed reaction at witnessing her partner's demise left her momentarily vulnerable as well, and Hyla took advantage of the opportunity. Launching her tongue again, the Amphibian embedded her spike in her target's throat, but was about to suffer a fate just as severe. Saddleback had turned just in time for a spiny cone jutting out from one of her shoulder blades to pierce Hyla's tongue, and the deadly poison took effect immediately. Each began to lose her respective grip and, as they fell, a powerful burst of kinetic energy suddenly exploded from the Rainbow Veil. The ship rocked, and the two nearly lifeless bodies disappeared into the grievous night.

The battle between Sir Albatross and Peregrine ground to a halt, and Peregrine knew the time had come to take his leave. With both of his allies defeated, he would have to retreat and resume his chivalrous duel with Sir Albatross another time. He bowed to his esteemed adversary, turned swiftly, and shot back through the Veil. The Crimson Crest entered moments later.

Chapter IV - A New Creation

King Eagle's broken heart weighed heavily as he resided in his solar, which was set apart from the main tower of Cloud Castle by a quaint arcade bridge. The Spirit of Phoenix Prime rested gently on him, comforting him as he sat in quiet contemplation and mourning. Through the prophetic window, he noticed things looked brighter outside, though he was yet unaware of Hyla and what had become of her. The Crimson Crest had entered once again into the world of Animystia, and his hope of the advent of Captain Cardinal carried him.

After he and Hyla had emerged for the battle on the Crimson Crest, Carnelian had taken Jack below again, to the wardrobe in the cabin of Captain Cardinal, and had instructed him to change into the outfit belonging to them that would accommodate their combined features. The ensemble had been a little awkward in his Tellurian state, but he trusted the bird, and he saw what the synthesis might look like in his mind.

His mental review had him wearing a pair of trousers and a buccaneer shirt, both of which were nearly the same hue as the feathers they were covering, the back of the shirt having fine slits for his wings; a red metallic breastplate, with a black diamond on its chest, designed to additionally protect his neck and shoulders; black leather gloves, accented by a single red diamond on the flap of each; and a pair of similarly fashioned boots, each of which had three toe holes in the front and one in the back, compensating for the mutated physiology of those extremities. To cap it all off, he was wearing a stylishly brimmed crimson chapeau.

Sir Albatross was distraught, blaming himself for Hyla no longer being with them, though he could not have controlled that outcome. Lord Peacock's heartache came from a deep resonance with Hyla's bravery in battle and her heroic sacrifice. Though they both had an idea about the one who was about to light the way, they were nevertheless awestruck when they first saw him, and it had even been sufficient to momentarily distract them from thoughts of their lost ally.

Upon passing through the Rainbow Veil, Captain Cardinal was now in full form. The bond between Carnelian and Jack Diamond had taken place, and the Tellurian's vision had been realized. Internally, all of the bird's wisdom, wit, and knowledge belonged to the new hybrid. Externally, he was coated with bright red plumage, with a crest of crimson adorning the crown of his head, and possessed the feathery means to fly. His stubby toes had been replaced by piercing talons, and a sharp reddish beak took the place of a soft human mouth. His brown eyes were enlarged, now accentuated by a jet-black mask.

The memory of Hyla soon returned when the Crimson Crest began to draw near to Volar and Cloud Castle was in sight. The absence of King Eagle there to greet them as they approached intensely amplified their shared grief. Nevertheless, there was someone there to welcome their return. When the ship docked on its custom platform, the pair of lords, along with their new companion, disembarked and were met by Lady Bluebird.

One of the Courtly Council, she was a beautiful Avian with a vivid deep blue cowl over a rusty throat. Hemmed in white, the color she wore matched her plumage, which lay beneath icy blue metallic armor. Through the window of the room in which she had concealed herself and another during the assault, she had gratefully seen the returning Crimson Crest approaching.

Beside her was a yellow-beaked juvenile male Avian about three and a half feet tall, whose name was Starling. His purplish-green iridescence radiated in the brilliant light of the moon, which had lost its bloody coloration. He was a ward of the castle, along with two other juveniles, who were in their quarters below when Mockingbird attacked. One of them was his young love interest, Rosy-Finch, whom everyone just called Rosy; the other, her overprotective brother, Brambling. When they had come up to investigate, Lady Bluebird was able to snatch Starling and get him to safety, but the other two were taken hostage.

Now Starling's excitement had overrode his propriety, and he gleefully declared the name of Captain Cardinal, whom he recognized standing in front of him. He had relatively little understanding of the prophecy, but he had been taught enough for his childlike faith to draw him heroic inspiration. Lady Bluebird put an arm around his shoulder and introduced him to their prophesied savior, who knelt down and offered a humble hand to shake. Starling went in for a hug, and the captain graciously hugged him back.

Meanwhile, the lady welcomed home the lords with a blend of relief, endearment, and desperation. Exchanging friendly honorable gestures with Sir Albatross, she said, "I'm glad you made it back safely, my lord. It's good to see you."

"It's good to see you," he returned.

She was, however, more delighted to see the one beside him. She and Lord Peacock were deeply in love and were pledged to be married. She didn't know about Hyla yet, but she could see he was hurting, and she wrapped her arms around him to ease his pain. He was far more grateful for her than he could show in that moment.

Meanwhile, the king was in his solar (from which he hadn't left since before their departure), and he was waiting to meet with them, particularly the new arrival. Lady Bluebird escorted them all across the lowered castle drawbridge and saw them to the arcade bride leading to the solar, where she stayed with the other two as the pair of lords went to retrieve the king.

"Sir Albatross, Lord Peacock, welcome home," King Eagle gratefully expressed, letting them in.

He and Sir Albatross embraced as beloved brothers, and they both wept. Lord Peacock was generally disinterested in hugging a male for any reason, so normally a hearty handshake would have been standard protocol for him. The moment the king turned to him, though, something broke; he crumbled into his majesty's arms, releasing a flood of emotion that seemed to have been amassing for a long time. The loss of Hyla, on top of everything else, was simply too much for him. Sir Albatross put his hand on his fellow lord's shoulder to comfort him as well.

"Was the mission successful?" the king asked the larger lord after some moments of their consolation.

"He is here," Your Majesty," Sir Albatross replied. "He is waiting for us with Lady Bluebird and Starling."

"Thank Phoenix Prime," the king declared. "But the mission was not all successful, was it, Lord Peacock?" he asked delicately. "What happened?"

Lifting his head to the king's compassionate countenance, the saddened noble winced at the sight of the golden-metallic patch over the cavity where the former's blown-out right eye used to be. King Eagle had lost nearly everything, yet he had put aside his own pain in order to give his friend solace.

"We had a stowaway on the ship," Sir Albatross began to explain. "Her name was Hyla, according to our new hero, and she gave her life to ensure that we made it."

Lord Peacock's tears showed the king that what she'd done had meant more to him than he could ever verbalize. "O, my dear Peacock, I understand," the king assured him. "May she rest in peace."

"Th-thank you," Lord Peacock replied appreciatively, his eyes drying.

"We will honor her along with my son, Prince Heron."

"Yes, my king," both lords answered simultaneously.

The three of them proceeded to rendezvous with the other trio on the bridge, Sir Albatross on King Eagle's right, and Lord Peacock on his left. Starling and the hulking lord stood apart from each other. The juvenile was around half Sir Albatross' height, and the contrast was striking. However, the gentle giant knelt, grinned, and made a fist for his young friend to pound. Starling slapped it instead, and his open hand barely covered it.

Lord Peacock once again found himself in the presence of his beloved bride-to-be. They took each other by the hands, still needless to speak. Captain Cardinal recalled a memory from Jack's life, and he appreciated what had been left behind. Attachments from his old life were still falling away, but he realized that even if he could go home, things were altogether different now. He was different now.

That left him and the king in the middle to make their acquaintance. "Captain Cardinal," the latter began. "I am King Eagle, but you already knew that," he chortled. "We are thankful you are here."

"I am thankful to be here," Captain Cardinal agreed.

The benevolent king looked on him approvingly, taking him in for several moments before clasping his shoulders, acknowledging, "At last, how welcome you are." Scanning through the windows of the new creatin's soul, the king recognized the manifestation of Phoenix Prime within him as Carnelian showing up in a twinkle of his eye. "Now, let us make it official," he declared.

Captain Cardinal, by knowledge of the incarnation within, had an awareness of what was about to take place, a ceremony in honor of his arrival and the commencement of his inheritance. Lady Bluebird and Starling crossed over and stood with the lords. The four of them each took a step backward and knelt in reverence.

When all were in place, the king commanded, "Kneel, Jack Diamond."

The foretold champion took the knee, but the part of him that was Jack felt slightly awkward. The Carnelian part quickened him, however, reminding him that this was his moment. Immediately, a great peace came upon him, and he felt released to close the book on his old life with finality and move fearlessly into the new.

"From this day forward," the king continued, "you shall no longer be called by that name." Withdrawing his regal sword majestically for the accolade, he pronounced, "Henceforth, you shall be called Captain Cardinal." At the declaration of his title, he touched the flat of his blade to the captain's right shoulder, and to his left at the mention of his likeness.

"I name you Captain of the Crimson Crest, the ship of your birthright, which you arrived in. Sir Albatross, Lord Peacock, Lady Bluebird, and Starling will be at your command. The treacherous traitor, Major Mockingbird, and his wayward cohorts threaten the freedom of the Northern Realm and all of Animystia. You are charged with defending that freedom at all costs. Rise now, Captain Cardinal, of Cloud Castle and the Crimson Crest."

When Captain Cardinal had stood to his feet again, King Eagle stepped across himself and stood with him at his right hand. Addressing the rest, he commissioned them, saying, "This is my servant, and he is your servant, for he is a servant of Phoenix Prime, who now dwells within him. Therefore, we shall honor and serve him as it is fitting. Our adversary is formidable, but we have the upper hand, for the one who is life and resurrection fights with us and for us. Join me in celebrating this gift of Phoenix Prime, Captain Cardinal!"

Shouts of praise and thanksgiving began, but quickly subsided as it was evident that Lord Peacock was still wounded by Hyla's altruism, which kept him from fully appreciating

Captain Cardinal for who he was. For a sign, the captain asked the king if he might lay a hand over the patch to restore his eye. Recalling that the prophecy spoke of bringing sight to the blind, faith entered the king's heart for healing, and he graciously allowed him.

Removing his right glove and giving thanks to Phoenix Prime, the captain stretched forth his hand and laid it over the wound. "Receive your sight, Your Majesty," he uttered with an untold authority.

Immediately, the king felt his cells reforming and new tissue being created. The captain removed his hand and put his glove back on. The king removed his patch, and the light gleamed from a brand new, fully functioning eyeball. Lord Peacock's hesitations completely vanished.

Chapter V - Mockingbird's Nest

Peregrine had meanwhile returned to the Isle of Bedim, and was now suffering the consequences of allowing his allies to perish and of failing to prevent Captain Cardinal from manifesting. Major Mockingbird's lieutenant, Razorbill, who had been one of the others with them at the insurrection, had been waiting for Peregrine upon his arrival. He was decked with dark steel armor; most of his plumage was jet black, but white from the collar down, and his sharp hatchet-shaped bill was black with a transverse white band.

Knowledge of what had taken place had already reached Mockingbird's ears, and he was entirely displeased with the outcome. Razorbill, also being rather spiteful, was all too satisfied to speculate at great lengths upon the severity of the punishment Peregrine would receive for his failure as he escorted him into the throne room of Mockingbird's Nest—an impenetrable dark metallic fortress. Peregrine had allied himself with the tyrant due to having lost confidence in King Eagle's leadership, but as he was made to kneel before the dark despot, he wished for a third option.

The Major's throne bore an uncanny resemblance to King Eagle's own seat of power. The only noticeable difference was that it was considerably more elevated, due to an unusual elaborate platform. As he sat upon it, he cruelly eyed the one with whom he was displeased. "Razorbill, leave us," he commanded, waving out his lieutenant.

"My lord," Razorbill pleaded.

"Fine, Razorbill," he relented, "you can bear witness to what happens when you fail me. As you are aware, I do not accept failure." He arose and stepped down from his throne, flexing his wings. "This is what happens when you fail me," he pronounced, perniciously grabbing Peregrine's left wing and yanking him to his feet with brute force, causing him to shriek, racked with excruciating pain.

Crossbill, one of Mockingbird's henchmen that had appeared on the offensive in Jack's apocalyptic dream, was looking on from the shadowed hallway with a fiendish curiosity as Peregrine dropped back to his knees. Lurking there with him were three other Avians. Two of them had intermittently held a seat on the Courtly Council; "Red" Bishop and the slate blue-winged Kestrel, who was known for his hovering ability. The third was Brambling.

While Crossbill reveled in the cruel environment, the other three were less enthusiastic. Bishop and Kestrel both had mixed feelings about Peregrine, but they at least respected him, and were appalled at the black-hearted mistreatment of him by someone who also once shared their title. They remained silent, but Brambling impulsively tore out of their hiding place in protest against the Major's actions, an act he would immediately regret.

"Crossbill!" Major Mockingbird screeched, recognizing the muffled sound of his evil cackling.

Bishop and Kestrel tried to sneak away, but Crossbill grabbed them both and forcibly shoved them into the audience chamber. He sauntered out behind them, while Brambling's hopes of unleashing his dagger against the Major were swiftly dashed.

"Apologies, my lord," Crossbill simpered.

Major Mockingbird fixed his attention on Bishop and Kestrel instead and demanded, "What do you two cowards have to say for yourselves?" Before either one managed to say anything, he ordered them in a threatening tone to remove themselves from his sight, and they took swift advantage of the opportunity.

He then ordered Crossbill concerning Brambling, "Take this annoying little brat and throw him in the dungeon."

"Come on," Crossbill growled, violently grabbing the juvenile's arms, which he proceeded to shackle. The elder miscreant then threw the younger over his shoulder and carried him out.

Once the uninvited company had all departed, Mockingbird returned to his throne and offered, "Now, Peregrine, I'm going to give you a chance to redeem yourself. After all, we are old friends."

Rage consumed Peregrine, who was increasingly regretful at having to serve this one he despised.

"Razorbill," Mockingbird barked, "take this disappointment and go to Ambrosia. Talk to the owner of the Pekin Duck, Mr. Mallard. He'll know you're coming."

"The 'restaurant' where we got the gun, my lord?"

"Yes, Razorbill," Mockingbird confirmed, producing a leather pouch full of gold coins, "his artificer has built us another advantage. Here is the payment he will require for it." He carelessly dropped the purse at his lieutenant's feet, and Razorbill knelt proudly, retrieving it. "Make haste, and return only when you have it," the Major ordered."

"As you wish, my lord," acknowledged his grim representative.

"And Peregrine," Mockingbird added sternly, "I can see the betrayal in your eyes. If you act on it, you will lose more than just a wing. Now, get out of my sight, both of you."

———

Brambling had been taken and locked in a tiny dingy prison cell in the catacombs below the keep. Lying supine on the hard stone floor due to the painfully low ceiling, he thought bitterly that his yellow beak's black tip might as well have been pressed up against it. He squinted his eyes, which were surrounded by buff rings, much like Captain Cardinal's. The accumulated grime from his enclosure had turned his orange and pale feathers nearly as dark as his black ones, and he grew darker inwardly as well, beginning to mutter curses.

"Who is there?" inquired a voice that was both instantly familiar and confusing.

"Queen Barbary?" he queried in astonishment.

"Brambling!" she cried, equally amazed.

"I thought you were dead," he said.

"No, thank the Maker," she replied. I've been held captive here ever since Lord Mockingbird betrayed us. He kidnapped me, and I found myself being interrogated by someone I once trusted with my life."

Brambling became even more disgusted with himself. He suddenly realized the irrationality of his negative attitude concerning the relationship between his sister and Starling, who should have been his best friend, and resolved to make things right if he ever escaped. Seeing the potential of molding them to his cruel will, Mockingbird had spared him and Rosy in exchange for their servitude. This was the worst treatment he had received so far, and it was his own fault. He fervently hoped the Major hadn't done any harm to Rosy on his account.
While he was internally processing these things, the queen said, "If my husband thinks I'm still alive, he must be worried."

"I think, deep down, he still has hope that you're alive," Brambling reassured her.

"Thank you, dear," she acknowledged.

Curious, he asked her, "Why did Mockingbird kidnap you and keep you alive? If he wanted to really hurt the king, wouldn't killing you have made more sense? I mean, I'm glad you're still alive, but… why?"

"Honestly, I have no idea," she wondered aloud. "After he interrogated me, he threw me in here, and I haven't seen or heard from him since."

Another voice answered quietly, "It's because you

have vital information that he will need in order to fully carry out his plans. That's got to be why he was interrogating you, but you must not have told him what he wanted to know. When he needs you again, he'll definitely come back for you. We must get you free now."

Brambling perked up and asked, "Rosy, is that you, sis?"

"Yes, brother," she answered, "it's me. I'm going to get you two out of here."   "Oh, Rosy, thank the Maker," Queen Barbary exclaimed.

As their would-be rescuer began messing with the locks, they heard approaching voices echoing in the hall. Brambling stopped her and exhorted her to get back to Cloud Castle and get help. She nodded that she understood and took off in the opposite direction of the echoes. As she found her way out, she passed by a room in which she saw a dismembered figure lying on an operating table, and she lamented for the king.

Chapter VI – The Grey Fox

A crippling rainstorm opened up on Rosy near the end of her predawn flight. It poured over Volar as thunder and lightning raged outside of Cloud Castle, whose occupants had all retired to rest for their impending mission. King Eagle was dreaming, and he saw a vision of the young one outside trying to get in. He heard the echo of a faint cry, either somehow through the wall or from within the dream, and awoke. Quickly getting up and opening the door to his external perch, he received the drenched and desperate young messenger. "Rosy," he whispered, and held her in his warm and comforting arms.

She was shivering, partly from the weather, and partly from the urgency of the news she needed to deliver. He breathed a sigh of relief for her return and, although he knew she had something of great importance to tell him, wanted to make sure her well-being was taken care of first. He carried her speedily to the kitchen and sat her down, then went back to the doorway. With an urgent cry, the residents of the castle were all in his presence within moments.

Inviting the rest into the kitchen, he directed Lady Bluebird to bring Rosy a warm blanket. The lady left immediately, returning promptly with a downy comforter in her arms. Lovingly, she draped it around the little one and wrapped her arms around her, giving thanks with joyful tears for her return. She loved Rosy like a sister.

The king addressed Lord Peacock, "We shall adjourn to the Three O'clock Room. Please prepare a meal for our dear Rosy, and join us when you have it ready."

"As you wish, my king."

"Sir Albatross, if you would be so kind as to carry her."

"Yes, Your Majesty," the muscular Avian replied as he gently scooped her up in the blanket.

She clung securely to his neck, with her head resting over his broad shoulder. Noticing Starling urgently trying to catch her attention, despite her weariness, she returned an affectionate smile. He could hardly believe she was back, and desperately longed to embrace her, but knew he would have to wait. Her unspoken sentiment, however, managed to put him at ease. He followed, along with King Eagle and Lady Bluebird, as Sir Albatross carried her to the designated room.

The Three O'clock Room was one of twelve named for the hands on a clock, which were arrayed in a circle, with the Twelve O'clock Room door at true north. The rooms of each sat above the corresponding thrones of their inhabitants, built into the castle wall. They were all set up identically with a nest-like bed, a fireplace, shelving, and a tall arched glass window with a golden lattice. Each window's sill sat just a few inches above the floor, and the halves of each opened inwardly to reveal a balcony with a wooden perch wide enough for two. A washroom with a smaller similar window and a large curtained bath was on the right, separated by a wooden door. The Twelve O'Clock and One O'Clock Rooms were the king and queen's respectively, and they were connected within.

In the main section of the Three O'clock Room, Sir Albatross delicately placed Rosy in the nest-bed and stood back with the king and Starling. As they waited for Lord Peacock and Captain Cardinal to arrive, Lady Bluebird settled down with Rosy and continued to comfort her. While they waited, it became apparent that Rosy couldn't any longer.

The king tenderly entreated her, "My daughter, please tell us what has happened, and under what conditions have you now returned to us?"

The young Avian was anxious and scared; looking down, she tightly gripped the blanket around her as tears began to flow from her weary eyes. What she knew, she wanted to reveal to the king, but felt ashamed. Guilt gnawed at her for having been aware of the truth while he wasn't. He knelt gently in front of her, lovingly took here by the hand, and took her into his fatherly embrace. She buried her face in his chest, and her muffled voice confirmed his deepest hope.

She continued sobbing, pleading, "Please don't be angry with me because I have shown more loyalty to my brother than to my king." While she wept, she failed to see the tears of delight in his eyes.

He lifted her sodden beak and spoke kindly. "Dear child, how could I be angry with you? My queen is alive, and you are home safe and sound. These are causes for celebration."

In the kitchen, meanwhile, Captain Cardinal had stayed back at Lord Peacock's request; the latter had invited the former to sit while he put on some leftover stew for Rosy. As it was reheating, he divulged to the captain the reason he had wanted a private audience. "How were you able to heal him?" he inquired.

"I know you're wrestling, Lord Peacock," the captain offered compassionately. "I myself am primarily a witness to how the prophetic promises made about me are unfolding. I just knew what needed to be done. The spirit of Phoenix Prime in me is confirming my testimony with signs and wonders, and we may get used to being astonished."

The lord stood and turned his back to the captain.

"What is it, Lord Peacock?"

He turned back around and demanded, "What about Hyla?"

The captain breathed a heavy sigh and replied, "Do not be burdened any longer, my friend. She is at peace. We will see her again in Uiribnar."
Lord Peacock suddenly felt lighter, and the captain gained a smile from his now less sorrowful companion. Afterward, they returned to the stew, which had heated up sufficiently. The lord composed himself and held out a bowl, while the captain took a ladle and dished it up. "Ready?" the captain asked when it was full.

Lord Peacock nodded in confirmation and, with

the bowl of food in his careful hands, they left the kitchen and began to ascend the spiral staircase that lined the cylindrical wall of the castle. The lord himself, although gorgeously plumed, was very limited in his flight, and there was a bit more he wanted to talk about on the way up. As they approached the door to the room in which the others were waiting, a curious light behind another door caught Captain Cardinal's peripheral attention.

"Go on ahead, I'll be right there," he said, and peeled off in the opposite direction.

Lord Peacock entered the Three O'clock Room and handed the bowl of stew to Lady Bluebird, who then lifted a spoonful of the savory morsels to Rosy's little beak. The king encouraged her to eat in order to regain her strength, and thanked both Lady Bluebird and Lord Peacock, then asked the lord concerning the whereabouts of Captain Cardinal.

"He said he'd be right here, but I..." Peacock trailed off.

Looking back through the door, he saw the captain standing on the ledge outside the door of the Nine O'clock Room. The latter was reading a note pinned thereto by an arrow and, as he pulled out the pointed shaft with one hand and removed the letter with his other, turned around. Meeting eyes with Lord Peacock, he beckoned him.

"What is it?" inquired the king.

"Not sure," Lord Peacock answered, "but it appears Captain Cardinal has found something. I'll be right back, Your Majesty."

Upon Peacock's having leaped and glided across the threshold, the captain immediately handed him the note, which read:

Two roles played, and two lives saved
Value both, and both shall stay
Judgments made for bygone ways
Killing one, them both with slay

The Grey Fox

"What do you think it means?" the lord asked the captain.

"I have a feeling we'll know once we enter this room," the latter answered.

King Eagle was looking on with anticipation, and caught the signal to join them. He and Sir Albatross left their assurances with the lady and the two young ones, and made their way swiftly across. Captain Cardinal read the note aloud at the king's request, who desperately hoped his son was behind the door, and gave the captain the nod to open it.

Through the slight crack at the bottom of the doorway, a greenish flickering luminescence was barely visible, which only added to the mystery. When the captain turned the handle and cracked the door, however, the emerald light suddenly disappeared. He proceeded to open the door cautiously and, by the moonlight shining in through the window, saw a figure he immediately perceived to be one of the lives the Grey Fox's cryptic letter made reference to. Looking over his shoulder, he gave Lord Peacock an encouraging nod, then stepped aside and allowed the lord to enter first.

"Hyla!" Lord Peacock gasped when he saw her tranquil body lying in the nest-bed, which was bathed in the subtle transition of lunar and solar light cast from the window, crisscrossed in thin shadow from the lattice.

"Hyla?" Sir Albatross queried with excitement, still outside the room. "She's alive?"

"Light the fireplace," Captain Cardinal suggested to the larger lord.

Once the room was aglow with the crackling fire, the captain approached Hyla to examine her. She was sleeping and, astoundingly, appeared to be in excellent health. Sir Albatross and the king entered the room in order to see her for themselves. There was a great prayer of thanksgiving initiated by the king, and they all delighted in the knowledge that their fallen comrade was actually alive and had been returned to them in apparently pristine condition.

The captain's attention returned to the puzzling parchment still in his hand. There was yet the matter of answering who the second life belonged to, and a logical idea suddenly presented itself to him. Understanding exactly where to find the answer, he turned resolutely to face the washroom door.

Chapter VII - Chrysalis

Sir Albatross noticed the tension as the others picked up on the captain's instinct and cautioned, "Remember what the note said. Two lives were saved. If one of them was our friend, whoever is in there will likely have been an enemy of ours."

"I believe you are right, Sir Albatross," King Eagle acknowledged.

The captain thoughtfully clenched the note in his fist.

The king paused to carefully consider his next words. "If whoever lies beyond this door is in fact known to us as an enemy," he concluded, "we will do no harm. If Phoenix Prime saw fit to use the Grey Fox to save this life as well, it must have been for a worthy reason. We thought we had already lost Hyla once. Let us pray we do not have to mourn for her again."

"King Eagle is right," the captain agreed. "We will be kind to her."

"It's the Lepidopteran, isn't it?" Sir Albatross inquired for confirmation.

"Yes," the captain attested. "The one who poisoned Hyla is in there."

"I suppose the Grey Fox could have somehow caught them both when they went overboard," Albatross concluded.

Along with the king, the two of them contemplated the matter silently.

Lord Peacock took the opportunity to interject his disgusted opinion, demanding, "Seriously, why? Why would anyone want to save a wretched thing like that?"

"Perhaps there is something we do not know," Sir Albatross offered. "We must be open to accept that things may not always be what they seem, my esteemed brother."

Lord Peacock was about to debate him, but the attention of everyone shifted to sounds of stirring from both Hyla and the suspect behind the washroom door. All eyes fell on the king for direction.

"Sir Albatross, "please be so kind as to check on Lady Bluebird and the juveniles, and return with them," he charged.

"Of course, my king," Albatross replied, leaving immediately.

The king addressed Lord Peacock.

"Yes, Your Highness," he replied.

"Please stay with and attend to Hyla."

"Thank you," the lord said.

To Captain Cardinal, the king decreed, "You and I shall unveil the truth of what lies behind this door."
The former grabbed the torch, and they nodded resolutely to one another.

As the captain reached for the door handle, the king stopped him, whispering, "I'll go first. We don't know what we're going to find in here, but if I can protect you, I will."

Bowing his head with gratitude, the captain honored the king's request and stepped aside, handing him the torch. The door opened to the right, so as King Eagle peeked in, his line of sight was pointing toward the bath to the left. Signifying to the captain that there seemed to be no immediate threat, he led the way in, placing the torch in the sconce fixed next to the entrance.

Meanwhile, Lord Peacock began to slowly take Hyla by the part of her hand which was covered by a fingerless orange glove. "Are you alright?" he regarded her gently.

Blinking, she adjusted to being awake, regaining consciousness fairly easily. "I think so," she supposed, quite confused.

"Thank Phoenix Prime," he acknowledged.

"Where am I?" she inquired. "How long have I been asleep? Am I in the king's castle? The last thing I remember... I was blacking out and falling."

While helping her to sit up, Peacock reassured her as best he could, "You nearly died while saving us from certain defeat, but you were somehow saved yourself by someone called the Grey Fox. We don't know how long you've been here, but we are indeed in the castle. We've only just found you, and thank Phoenix Prime you are alive. When you went overboard, we desper... I desperately wanted to land and search for you, but we were forced to return immediately..."

Her smile and gently voiced gratitude warmed his heart, and he allowed himself to breathe.

She pondered aloud, "The Grey Fox...?"

Sir Albatross returned just then with the lady and the little ones, and Hyla's query triggered a memory in his mind. He got their attention, saying, "I've just re-membered where I've heard that name before. Someone shared the ancient legend with me a long time ago, but I'd forgotten about it."

"What legend?" Hyla and Lord Peacock both inquired.

"It's a story that dates back probably to the beginning of civilization on Animystia. Some say they are a clan of ninja. Others claim there is just one that is either immortal or passes the title on. Either way, the Grey Fox is not to be taken lightly. We are most fortunate that he —"

"Or they," Lord Peacock cut in.

"Or they," Sir Albatross continued, speaking to Hyla, "chose to rescue you, but he—"

"Or they," Starling echoed playfully.

"Or they, thank you," Albatross smiled, patting the juvenile on the head, "also rescued one of our adversaries."

––––––––––––

The conversation ended as Captain Cardinal popped his head through the doorway and politely interrupted them, exhorting, "Lords, come quickly, you're not going to believe this."

The captain and the king had only been in the next room for a few moments. Upon entering, they'd stood before the veil separating the mysterious whimpering creature from their sight, contemplating their next move.

"What do you think?" Captain Cardinal had asked the king.

"I'm not sure, but have your blade ready," the latter had replied."

Grasping the hilt of his sword, the captain had been ready to draw it, while the king had prepared to draw back the curtain. Nodding again in agreement, the king had removed the thin visual blockade, revealing a great surprise to them both. What they'd beheld hanging in front of them was an intricately designed chrysalis of dazzling multi-colored beauty. They'd marveled as the pupa wriggled inside her cocoon, preparing to emerge for her second stage of life.

———————

Presently, Lord Peacock and Sir Albatross swiftly responded to the urgent beckoning of Captain Cardinal. Joining with him and the king in the washroom, they began discussing the perplexing sight. Still in the other room, Lady Bluebird noticed the challenging poetic letter the captain had left behind, and picked it up to investigate it. She read it aloud to Hyla, Rosy, and Starling.

All recognizing that Hyla was one of the lives saved, the Amphibian herself began to flare up at the thought of who the other was. Hearing faint dialogue through the wall, merciless thoughts flooded her mind. If she had been on the other side of the divide in that moment, she might have let murder have its victory.

"Hyla," Lady Bluebird said gently, "This seems very personal for you, and I can feel your anger, but we can't kill whomever is in there."

Hyla's vexation began to subside, knowing the lady had spoken correctly, as well as secretly remembering a promise.

"Whatever she's done to you," the lady continued, "it seems that the condition of your survival is that we allow you both to live. It may not make sense right now, but I'm sure Phoenix Prime has a good plan for her."

"I hope you're right," Starling piped up.

"I think we're actually in for a pleasant surprise, " Rosy posited enthusiastically. "Come on!" she shouted, grabbing Starling by the hand, sprinting toward the door. While the others worked out what she was alluding to, she grabbed the handle and burst in through the door, capturing the attention of the king, the captain, and the lords. "Thought so," she said to Starling as she spotted the writhing pupa.

"What is it, young one?" the king inquired.

"Yes, tell us," the captain encouraged.

"Well, King Eagle, Captain Cardinal," Rosy began, pointing to the inhabited chrysalis, "I heard them talking about her. I was thinking, you know, Saddleback was one thing before… well, they said she's going to be something different when she comes out of… well… that thing." She pointed at the chrysalis. "Maybe she could be our friend."

"I disagree with the possibility that she should be considered anything less than hostile," Lord Peacock suggested, partaking in a feeling of necessity to avenge Hyla, making Rosy frown.

"Thank you for your concern, Lord Peacock," the king reassured him. "Remember, it's not for us to take vengeance into own hands. That's the coward's route, the route Mockingbird took. You are not a coward, Lord Peacock."

A moment of tender silence passed for everything to sink in, then the king continued, "I think young Rosy here has the right idea. There is a larger picture here which we don't have all the pieces of, one sometimes our young can see more of. As we know, not all transformations are bad." He indicated Captain Cardinal, giving him esteem.

"Thank you, my king," the captain said graciously. "I agree with the youthful sentiment of hope concerning this new creature. Let her be received as I was."

With Saddleback's neoteric form about to come forth, they bowed their heads in reverence, and the king began to lead them in prayer. "O great and powerful Phoenix Prime, Spirit of life and peace, we give you honor and glory and thanks. All things come from you, and this creation is no exception. Therefore, you love her no differently than you love any one of us. Give us the grace to forgive her past and, through us, provide for her the surroundings for a better future. We trust that you have good plans for her, and we ask that you might present her to us as an ally and a sister. We thank you for bringing Rosy home to us and for protecting our loved ones who are still in captivity. Strengthen our hearts. Amen."

CHAPTER VIII - GOOD FOR BUSINESS

Leaving Mockingbird's Nest in order to carry out their forced assignment, Razorbill and Peregrine hurriedly approached their transport, which was similar to the one Saddleback and Yellowjacket had used. There was an uneasy tension between the two, as Peregrine was justifiably angry at Razorbill for the way he had "greeted" him upon his return. Razorbill was not exactly a fool, and though he didn't care at all how Peregrine felt, he wanted to get the job done with as little obstruction as possible. Therefore, he feigned an apology, but the familiar feeling of insincerity annoyed Peregrine even more, and he kept silent.

"Look, we have a job to do," Razorbill said roughly. "Get over it."

If Peregrine wasn't in such a weakened and despondent state, he likely would have knocked his rude accomplice out cold. Rather, he clenched his beak instead of his fists, and held his peace.

"I'll drive," Razorbill volunteered sarcastically.

Once they had mounted and Razorbill had prepared the vehicle for departure, they took off in the direction of Ambrosia. It was a significant distance from Bedim, and day had already well broken by the time they arrived. Also known as the Ambrosian Isle, Ambrosia was longer than any other island in the Animystian sky, and they had to scan for several minutes before finally locating the Pekin Duck. The restaurant's enormous hand-painted yellow, red, and green sign gave it away.

While they circled around to the docking side of the island, Razorbill noticed a cloudship stationed there with a light-purplish shade of blue—like that of a clear, unclouded sky. He considered its peculiarity, and he wondered who might have commissioned it. However, he let the thought of it pass as he shifted his attention toward the one vacant speeder platform.

Landing a fair distance away from the restaurant, Razorbill quickly dismounted, and he surveyed his surroundings as he waited impatiently for Peregrine to depart the craft. The latter took his time, partly out of pain and partly to annoy his colleague. Finally making it over to the spacious patio dining area, they found themselves an empty table and sat down inconspicuously. Razorbill placed a golden coin with Mr. Mallard's head on it at the edge of the table, and the two Avians then picked up their menus, pretending to read them while they waited.

Only a handful of moments passed before a fairly young Avian female gracefully glided through the open entryway from the inside portion of the restaurant. She was petite, with a sleek head and torso the color of midnight. Her wings were a cascade of bright cool colors, and her tail feathers were rimmed with jungle green. Her smile was sharp, and her teeth were sharper, which were offset by her remarkably pleasant greeting and overall demeanor.

"Hello boys, name's Tryxie. Be taking care of you fine-feathered fellas this evening. What can I get you…

oh," she interrupted herself, noticing the coin. She immediately narrowed her eyes, which were small but bright red, and put her notepad and writing tool in her apron. Otherwise, the change in her demeanor was imperceptible. "Follow me," she advised, and casually strolled back inside.

Razorbill nudged Peregrine's arm, and the latter begrudgingly got up and followed him as he followed Tryxie. She made sure they were behind her, but not so as to attract the wrong kind of attention, and they kept pace. She took them through a set of doors labeled "PRIVATE" and into a narrow hallway with a mostly viridian striped motif. Halfway down the hall, she stopped at a door which was all green. As she held up her fist to knock, the door swung open, and her knuckles hit nothing instead.

Exiting the room was a charismatic Avian whose feathers reminded Razorbill of the lazuline ship outside. Though Mockingbird's minion could not have known, the character's build and height were nearly identical to Captain Cardinal's. If the enigmatic Avian hadn't been wearing a particularly stylish hat, which was much like a bluish version of the crimson captain's, another striking similarity would have been apparent. His crest would have been nearly indistinguishable against the ship that clearly belonged to him. He wore shades of blue as well, with black and white accents, that made him look like a distinguished pirate. Firmly grasped in his right hand was a silver case with a strange wing-like design etched into it. He politely excused himself as he passed through, exchanging a low-profile romantic gesture with Tryxie, which the dispirited but keen-eyed Peregrine perceived with mild curiosity.

As the cool stranger strolled down the hall, a cordial voice from inside the room beckoned, "Come in, Tryxie. Have our guests arrived?"

"Yes, Sir, Mr. Mallard," she dutifully confirmed, and she ushered Razorbill and Peregrine into the room, waiting respectfully in the doorway until she was gratefully dismissed with a polite gesture.

An authoritative fellow dressed finely in striped silken clothing, with a dark lustrous green head, stood from behind his desk and proceeded to greet his customers. "Ah, welcome gentlebirds. You must be Major Mockingbird's boys."

Razorbill nodded.

"Razorbill, I take it?"

Razorbill nodded again.

"Shall we get down to business then?" the proprietor suggested.

Mockingbird's lieutenant removed the sack of gold from his garb and inquired, "I take it you and Major Mockingbird have already discussed this transaction in full?"

"Indeed, we have," Mr. Mallard replied. "Your ship is ready and waiting."

"I'm guessing it's not the one we saw coming in?"

"Oh no, that ship belongs to Captain Blue Jay, whom you just saw leaving."

Razorbill raised his eyebrows and probed, "Captain Blue Jay?"

"Yes, Razorbill, he and I have a long-standing business relationship," Mr. Mallard explained, "Rest-assured, I am no respecter of Animystians. Whoever keeps me in business is… my business."

"Is our ship faster?" Razorbill pried.

Mr. Mallard gave a hearty laugh and said, "Razorbill, my friend, I wager it's as fast as your friend here used to be."

A nerve had been struck, and the target of the distasteful comment raised his eyebrows. He still wasn't in the mood to raise contention, though, so he took it in stride.

Razorbill set the payment on the desk, and Mr. Mallard pulled out a drawer. Retrieving from it the blueprints and instructions for operations and maintenance of the ship, he replaced them with the money pouch.

As Razorbill received the materials, he realized he had seen one custom ship on the island and only one. "Where is our ship?" he sharply inquired.

"It is being stationed on an island not far from here. Here are the coordinates," Mr. Mallard said matter-of-factly, handing Razorbill another piece of paper.

"Why isn't it here?" the latter necessitated. "How do we know we can trust you?"

"Now, now, Razorbill, my friend," the shrewd entrepreneur countered convincingly, "if I were to swindle you, that wouldn't be very good for business, would it?"

Razorbill reluctantly conceded, and Peregrine nodded in agreement.

"Very well, then," Mr. Mallard concluded. "May I show you out?

———————————

Meanwhile, Tryxie had already left the island herself, along with Captain Blue Jay, after having left Mockingbird's intermediaries with her employer. She was now conversing with another feathered female aboard the captain's brand-new cloudship, with whom she was now being acquainted. They were hitting it off and, in their brief introduction, Tryxie was sharing with her new colleague about her job at the restaurant.
"Did anything interesting happen there today?" the latter inquired.

"Well, Canary, my boss actually uses the restaurant as a front for other dealings..." She paused for effect.
"Oh," Canary gasped. "Yeah?"

"Mhm. Right before I got off," Tryxie continued, "I ended up taking these two mean-looking goons to meet him. Actually, one wasn't so bad, but he looked badly hurt and like he didn't really want to be there. I could tell. Anyway, I overheard something about another cloudship and someone nefarious named Major Mockingbird!" She contorted her face and made a ridiculous gesture with her hands, making fun of his name.

"Mockingbird!" Canary gasped again, her excitement leaving her.

"You know him?" Tryxie asked, surprised but curious.

"I used to..." she began, sullenly trailing off, but Tryxie's quizzical expression prompted her to go on. "He used to be one of us, but he betrayed us."

"Who's us?"

"We've only just started to know each other, haven't we, Tryxie?" she admitted, reflecting with mixed emotions. "He and I were both noble representatives of the Northern Realm, serving right alongside the once great King Eagle. I was called Lady Canary."

"'Lady Canary,' that does have a nice ring to it," Tryxie chortled.

"Thank you, Tryxie," the former lady replied in a kind of melancholy way.

"Oh, he's the one we're up against," Tryxie vocalized, suddenly making the connection.

"Up against?" Canary squawked, her yellow feathers getting ruffled.

"Yeah, we're joining up with... wait, you don't know the mission?" Tryxie was puzzled.

"Well... Captain Blue Jay found me running, and his confidence in my protection and provision if I joined his crew was all I needed at the time. I didn't realize we were running right back to face Mockingbird."

"Maybe you got away so you could help us fight?" Tryxie suggested.

"You know what, Tryxie? Maybe you're right," Canary agreed. "I'm done running."

"Of course, I'm right," Tryxie teased."

"To think, maybe you should have been on the Council?" Canary suggested.

"I like you," said Tryxie.

"I like you," said Canary, and they chortled delightfully.

Tryxie joked, "My Baby Blue told me he'd encountered Mockingbird once or twice before and didn't take too kindly to him either. He always thought there was something… off."

"'Off' is an understatement," Canary ridiculed, "he's gone completely mad."

"Mad, did you say?" came a jovial voice from behind.

Spinning around in tandem, Canary and Tryxie saw the one Peregrine had spied the latter trading covert kisses with leaning against the ship's mast and grinning comically.

"Captain Blue Jay!" they joyfully exclaimed.

"You want to see mad," he teased. "I left a little surprise in the way of sabotage, and those fine-feathered fellas you showed to Mr. Mallard's office earlier are heading right this way. We're about to have a little fun. What do you say, ladies?"

Adopting his playful expression, Tryxie and Canary glanced at each other, winked, and declared, "We're in!"

CHAPTER IX - THE COBALT CLOUD

The previously efficient aircraft transporting Razorbill and Peregrine suddenly began to choke and sputter. Panic gripped the pilot as he began to lose control, and expletives spewed from his mouth as he tried to regain it. Nothing was visible in the expanse of sky before them, other than an oddly placed patch of cloud, which was no place for a landing. Peregrine popped an eye open, concerned because of his inability to fly with only one wing. Razorbill's only thoughts were on the ship's paperwork and, desperately hoping not to fail, made sure it was on his person and within his grasp.

At the point it became apparent that regaining control of the vehicle was an impossibility, something solid appeared as a hole began to form in the cloud patch. Having no other option, Razorbill guided them toward the visible part of what was hidden behind the white fluffy facade. The object brilliantly reflected the afternoon sun, like a shining sapphire, and a feeling of apprehension swept over both of them. Suddenly, a hole opened up from it, and a cannon stuck out. In the fleeting moments before their vehicle was smashed to pieces by the cannonball, the struggling pilot realized they were heading for the cloudship he'd seen at the restaurant.

In shock and terror, Peregrine spun out of control, trying to stay airborne, while Razorbill struggled to help him. They were suddenly and swiftly snatched out of their panicked freefall by a massive rope net, and thick ropes cushioned their fall as they were deposited carelessly onto the hard wooden surface of the ship's deck. The blanket of white kept hidden from them all but the bluish planks beneath their bruised faces.

The precarious silence was pierced by the distinct sound of a gun hammer being cocked. Both Razorbill and Peregrine wished they each had their own personal firearm, never mind both of them being totally unarmed presently, as their swords were lost with the speeder. Echoing through the fog, the next thing they heard was a brash feminine voice shouting, "Clear!"

Within moments, the remaining cloud matter totally dissipated, revealing five other individuals. The captives both expected to see the blue-feathered Avian that had made his cameo with them in the hallway of Mr. Mallard's office, but they saw instead among the colorful crew the young female who'd taken them back there. If it wasn't enough of a shock to see Tryxie on board, it certainly was to have her aggressively pointing a loaded weapon at them.

Noticeably the ringleader of a fairly menacing crew, she brazenly encircled the on-edge prisoners and began to move in for the kill. Peregrine had already been captured once that day, and the fear of something happening to his other wing enveloped him. One of the approaching figures captured his shaky attention and, though quite confused, he was somehow a little comforted by her presence there. His time to reflect was cut short, however, as swords began slashing and cutting the net in a seemingly chaotic fashion. In the aftermath, Peregrine and Razorbill were both free of their captivity and somehow completely unscathed.

Tryxie uncocked her pearly pistol, whirled it around her finger, and let it slide neatly into its blue velvet holster. She couldn't contain herself any longer and burst out laughing hysterically. While her mates joined in, the bewildered Peregrine and Razorbill shared a look of mutual frustration and relief. Another grand voice quickly joined the entertained chorus, and all heads looked up to see Captain Blue Jay perched above his cabin door, chortling gleefully. From sheer enjoyment, he almost lost his balance and fell off the ledge, but righted himself dramatically.

Peregrine and Razorbill both failed to see the humor in the situation, but the former noticed amidst their vexation that Captain Blue Jay had something familiar in his hand. Since his own flight anatomy had been irreparably damaged, the wing design etched into the metallic case had left a distinct impression. Throwing caution to the wind, he stood up and suspiciously eyed the captain, curious about what would happen next. Taking his cue, Razorbill stood as well to join what he thought was a move of defiance.

Impressed with Peregrine's boldness, Captain Blue Jay alighted from the ledge and waltzed over to him, extending his hand. "Peregrine, I presume? It is truly an honor to personally meet you. Big fan." The subject of his introduction looked nonplussed, so he recovered with,

"Oh, pardon me, my friend. I suppose I should introduce myself. I am Captain Blue Jay, this is my crew, and this is my ship." He made the indications as he spoke, and Peregrine thought to himself the captain needn't waste his time explaining. The persistent captain continued, though, pretty much ignoring Razorbill as he went on to apologize to Peregrine for the way he had been brought on board. "As you can tell," he confessed, "we like to have a bit of fun on the..."

As he drew a blank, Tryxie sidled up to next to him, and he wrapped an affectionate arm around her. "Baby, what did we decide to call it?"

"The Cobalt Cloud," she chirped cheerfully.

"The Cobalt Cloud," he echoed with the same delight. "Anyway, I always say, 'If you can't have fun, what's the point,' right Tryxie?"

"That's right, Baby Blue," she agreed, giving him an adoring squeeze.

"That's right," he echoed playfully.

She then apologized herself to Peregrine. "I hope you're not upset with us. We really mean you no harm."

"Unless you intend to harm any of us," Captain Blue Jay added, addressing both Peregrine and Razorbill, sternly pointing his finger at Razorbill specifically. His tone and mannerisms left both of them wondering whether or not he was being facetious.

After another unsettlingly lingering moment, the captain let go of his girl. "Tryxie, dear?"

"Yes, Baby?"

Indicating Razorbill, he bid, "See to it that our other guest here stays entertained. Our friend Peregrine and I have an important matter to discuss."

Peregrine had no idea what the inscrutable captain meant by that, but he assumed it had something to do with the case in his hands. Cautious, he nevertheless accepted the captain's invitation to retire with him into his quarters. Captain Blue Jay casually thrust open his cabin door and allowed Peregrine the polite courtesy of first entry, corresponding with a nod.

Closing the door behind him and locking it, they proceeded to the back end of the room, and the captain propped the mysterious case up on the desk. Clicking the locks, he carefully opened it, revealing something Peregrine was completely unprepared for. His dumbfounded eyes beheld a pair of what almost looked like his wings, but of a dark-bluish metallic nature.

"What am I looking at?" Peregrine wondered aloud.

"These are your new wings, my friend," Captain Blue Jay answered him appreciatively.

"My new wings?" Peregrine suddenly became suspicious and sharply demanded, "What is this about, and why are you calling me friend? I don't know you."

"Ahhh, yes, but I know you," the captain replied. "Well, I know a fair bit about you at least. It is truly an honor to finally meet the Lord Peregrine in person. I saw how you recognized one of my crew, and I understand the two of you briefly served Eagle together?"

"Lady Canary," Peregrine recalled aloud.

"It's just 'Canary,'" the captain corrected, "like you apparently call yourself just 'Peregrine' now." He shook his head and changed the subject back, indicating, "Anyway, there is a set of wings here—"

"I only have one broken wing," Peregrine cut him off. "How's that going to work? Are you planning to break my other wing?" He actually made himself laugh, delighting in his own quick wit. Aerial velocity wasn't the only thing he was accelerated in.

Captain Blue Jay chuckled in response and replied, "No, no, of course not, Peregrine, we don't need to do that. In fact, I had Merlin design these according to your specs, one for the right wing and one for the broken left wing that will modify itself as you heal to compensate for strength. They will balance you out and give you back your flight. What's more, they will make you even faster than you were before that gift was shamefully stolen from you."

"Faster?"

Despite wondering how this charismatic stranger had acquired his measurements, the captain had Peregrine's undivided attention. His speed was what he was known for, and his pride could be restored now. He had already been the fastest in the sky, and he was elated at being presented the reality of not only being able to fly again, but even faster.

"Faster," the captain replied matter-of-factly.

Peregrine reverted to suspicion again and insisted,

"Wait a minute, why are you doing this? What's in it for you?"

Captain Blue Jay answered respectfully, "My dear Peregrine, I am doing this because you and I have the same goal. We are on the same side. We're going to kill Major Mockingbird."

Peregrine needed to hear no more. By whatever means his new unlikely ally had assumed his discontinued allegiance to Mockingbird and accompanied desire for revenge was irrelevant. He was looking at a formidable partner with undeniable resources, and he was sold.

Razorbill, meanwhile, was not being "entertained" as per Captain Blue Jay's ambiguous request. His skin crawled, ruffling his feathers, at the enjoyment Tryxie and the others were having at his expense. If given the chance, he would have unmercifully and unremorsefully gutted all of them, such was his disdain. However, being at their mercy, he settled for a less overt option and was playing along with the capricious crew as he had tried to do with Peregrine on their trip to Ambrosia. He had a bit more success with them because they were far less aware of his conniving nature.

While the rest of the crew antagonized him, an eccentric Avian male was tinkering with an aircraft that looked fairly similar to the one Razorbill and Peregrine had come in on. The hood of his shimmery spider-silk cloak, which draped neatly between his folded grey wings, was up over his head, closing off distraction while he worked. He was called Merlin, but his uncanny industrial prowess had earned him "The Wizard" for a nickname; his "magic touch" could fix, modify, or fabricate any technology.

While the others kept an eye on Razorbill, Razorbill kept an eye on Merlin. Thinking how perfectly he was being set up for a clean getaway, the former determined that once the latter had finished working, he would make his move. He originally thought he'd have to distract the lot in order to stealthily acquire the aircraft and escape before anyone was the wiser. Conveniently for him, as soon as the technician had put on the finishing touches, a shattering crack apprehended everyone's attention, and immediately the Cobalt Cloud began being swallowed up in the very same fog-like substance that had previously masked its appearance.

Merlin's hood flew back, and he shrieked, "The hydrogen gas!"

Razorbill considered how he himself wouldn't have been able to set it up better if he had tried. He seized his opportunity, seized Merlin, and snatched the keys. Casting the artificer violently aside and seizing the aircraft, he sped off in the obscurity and confusion. The genius Avian's vehicle was lighter and faster than his had been, and he fancied only Peregrine (if he could fly) could have caught up to him.

CHAPTER X - EMERGENCE

Meanwhile at Cloud Castle, the colorful chrysalis hanging in the Nine O'clock Room's washroom was being breached. Its occupant had reached her time of emergence, and she was entering the waking world once again. King Eagle and his allies waited with anticipation as they prepared for either reception or restraint. After several intense moments, the fully transformed Saddleback finally freed herself from her temporary imprisonment. She climbed down and stood delicately, stretching her new powdery wings. She gazed at her marveling audience, herself full of wonder.

Much to their relief, there appeared to be no hint of hostility or apparent cause for alarm. With the creature's physiology completely changed, the awkward and deadly protrusions she previously possessed were no longer there to rob her of comfort and make for her enemies. Her patterns were less extravagant, and her colors were duller, but there was a certain light of innocence that illumined her appearance. Though new in every way, she retained access to her larval memories, which gave her compassion.

Lady Bluebird was still in the main part of the room with Hyla and, recalling this, Lord Peacock excused himself politely and returned to the pair of females. Hyla saw a bit of disgust on his face and reacted impulsively. Leaping and flipping upside down, she affixed herself to the ceiling. She noticed her unique weapon that had been carefully placed in a cubby hole, and lashed her tongue out for it. Being armed made her feel more in control of the situation.

"Hyla, it's fine," Lord Peacock reassured her. "She's not a threat. I know what she did to you, but she's totally different now."

"I don't care," she argued. "She killed me!"

"I get that, Hyla, but Phoenix Prime saved both of you. Not to mention—"

"Lord Peacock," Lady Bluebird softly interjected, "give her a minute. I'll go talk to the others."

Departing from them and entering the washroom, she implored Captain Cardinal and King Eagle, "My Lieges, Hyla is still experiencing hostility, and your counsel is needed."

"Thank you, Lady Bluebird," the king commended her. "We will sort it out."

"Thank you, Your Majesty," she replied.

"Sir Albatross, take the young ones here and go begin preparations for our mission to rescue our queen and this dear one's wayward brother," he said, patting Rosy paternally on her downy head.

The faithful lord did as he was commanded, and the remaining three contemplated what to do.

"I should talk to her." Saddleback volunteered gently, taking them all by surprise.

Captain Cardinal studied her.

"Do you think that's a good idea, Captain?" the king asked.

The captain looked at him, then at her again, then at him again. "Yes, let her do it." he confirmed. "They both need it,"

The king was in agreement and suggested, "Lady Bluebird, bring her out momentarily. The captain and I will go out first and prepare Hyla."

"As you wish, Your Majesty," the lady replied.

The king and the captain exited the washroom, finding Hyla still secured defensively above them.

"Hyla," Captain Cardinal said graciously, "I'm very glad to see you're alive."

At the calming sight of him, she reservedly returned her trusty weapon to its resting place, then effortlessly dropped back to the nest-bed.

Grateful that the door had been opened to him, the captain acknowledged her disgruntled feelings and assured her, "You made it possible for me to be here, and I owe my life to you. We all do."

"All of Animystia does," Lord Peacock emphatically agreed.

The captain went on, imploring, "She has forgiven you and wants to tell you so herself, if you'll let her. Will you allow her to, and will you find your way to forgive her yourself?"

Hyla loved Captain Cardinal for the compassionate way he spoke. Her lime green countenance brightened, and she blushed when she realized she was in the favorable presence of the king as well. The door cracked behind him, and Lady Bluebird peaked her head out.

"Bring her out," the benevolent king encouraged.

The lady obliged and opened the door the rest of the way, allowing Saddleback to step out into the view of the tentatively receptive Hyla. The Amphibian saw that the Lepidopteran standing there with twitching wings was truly sorry and, suddenly feeling the same compassion, offered with joyful tears her own sincere apology.

CHAPTER XI - THE MASKED MIMIC

It was evening when Razorbill arrived at the provided coordinates in order to achieve possession of the ship he had been promised for Major Mockingbird. He began to approach what appeared to be an abandoned junkyard, but because of his recent encounter, he was more cautious while looking for a place to land. As he descended, the thought occurred to him that he might have been hoodwinked, because if there was a brand-new cloudship there awaiting his reception, certainly no evidence of it was apparent.

From what seemed like a field of inanimate objects, he saw small movements of dusty prospectors here and there, illuminated by the field lighting. As he drew closer, he saw waving him down a plump, blackish-brown and sparsely-haired Animystic with a large head and a formidable pair of tusks. Following the direction of the Swine's cloven hoof, he put down in a somewhat open area nearby. Dismounting disdainfully, he stepped away from his aircraft to engage the bizarre industrialist.

"Welcome," the stranger squealed, chewing on an elongated green vegetable. "What brings you to my Junkpen?"

Razorbill noticed the mechanical boneyard's sign confirming its name. He started to approach the owner threateningly, changing his approach when he realized how intimidating the Swine actually was up close. He allowed the odd bumpy-faced Animystic to continue his introduction.

"I'm Phaco, and all this is mine," he oinked braggingly.

Razorbill masked his impatience with difficulty.

"My assistant is currently off-grounds, but you may help yourself to what you need, if you have the tools," Phaco continued, glancing over the modest aircraft; not seeing any, he gave what he had thought to be a prospective buyer a baffled look.

"I don't see it," Razorbill said sharply.

"Oh," Phaco snorted, "you're here for the Masked Mimic?"

"The what?"

"Mr. Mallard sent you?"

"Yes, where is Major Mockingbird's ship?"

"The Masked Mimic," the Swine emphasized, "is right over there." He pointed at what seemed like an arbitrary mountain of parts and debris.

"I don't see anything," Razorbill snarled.

"I know," Phaco squealed. Subtly revealing a mechanism related to its functionality located on his person, he cryptically answered, "She can be made to look like anything you want her to."

"Phaco, was it? Do you know what this is?" Razorbill threatened, peeling back his black garb to showcase a weapon similar to that which Mockingbird had used to besiege Cloud Castle. Though he had lost his sword in the void beneath the Cobalt Cloud, he had delightfully discovered a gun and its holster on his new transport.

Fear manifested in Phaco's eyes, and he trembled visibly. "To my chagrin," he lamented. "My assistant is a genius, but at quite a cost, it seems. He's given us a cursed kind of power. Politics and kingdoms have no interest for the likes of us, only money. We are impartial inhabitants of these skies, and this was a job, one I'm not proud of..." he trailed off.

"Where's the ship?" Razorbill demanded, reaching for his firearm.

Rage kicked in, adding to the fear and regret. Phaco started to charge Razorbill, but the latter was too quick for him; the treacherous Avian pivoted to the side, drew his weapon, cocked it, and maliciously fired a shot. Fortunately for the stampeding Swine, the bullet happened to only snap off one of his tusks, though the pain infuriated him all the more.

The shot had answered the attempted murderer's question, though, when it ricocheted into a metallic surface on the fringe of what he thought was just a hulking junkpile. Looking again closer at where Phaco had originally indicated, he actually did see a ship, but it was camouflaged. While he began to inspect the now somewhat noticeable shape and form of the ambiguous object, he heard a defiant snort. Phaco had recovered quickly and was preparing to charge again. Razorbill cocked his gun again, unperturbed as the Swine gained momentum. Just before impact, the murderer leapt over Phaco, and shot him in the back.

While looting the lifeless body, Razorbill found

the device on the landlord he'd expected to find. It displayed a holographic image reminiscent of the way the undercover ship looked. He pressed a button on the device that made the image vanish, both on the device and on the cleverly disguised vessel. Uncloaked, he judged the latter's color scheme to be reminiscent of Mockingbird's coat of feathers, and it was comparable in size to the Cobalt Cloud.

"Intriguing," he thought aloud, and pressed another button that was self-explanatory based on the icon, lowering a cabin door from the side of the ship. Using observational logic again, the pressing of another series of buttons took him through a myriad of disguises for the stealth vessel, and he settled on one that made it indistinguishable from the night sky.

As Razorbill reached the muted fringes of Bedim, he was uncharacteristically nervous. He already knew that Major Mockingbird would consider Peregrine not returning with him a failure, and he was very clear on his overlord's methods of punishment. He was likewise aware that his imperious master would have had them followed and that he would no doubt have had the report of Peregrine's abandonment by now. It also dawned on him that Mockingbird would have learned of his recent murder, and that he would assuredly be demanding the surrender of the gun to his own possession, to say the least. The successful retrieval of the ship, he hoped, would at least be enough to quell the wrath that he feared would come upon him.

The doors of an underground hangar that had recently been constructed to house the vessel began to open as he brought it in. Razorbill began to speculate whether Mockingbird would be awaiting him there or in his throne room. Either way, the music would have to be faced. Descending through the opening, he saw the autocrat awaiting him there on the platform. To the servant's surprise, there seemed to be a somewhat amused expression on the Major's face.

Upon disembarking, Razorbill immediately prostrated himself before his sovereign. "Forgive me, my lord. I know that I have disappointed you. Peregrine—"

"Rise, Razorbill," Mockingbird instructed, cutting him off. "I am aware of your failures. Nevertheless, you have proven yourself a faithful and moderately useful servant. You even came here willingly to face me, without pretense, knowing that it might cost you your life. As for Peregrine, he will soon be dealt with. It is a shame about the Swine, but that hog got what was coming to him. Now what was his is mine."

Razorbill sensed Mockingbird was allowing him an opportunity to speak, so he ventured to confirm, "Then you are not going to deal harshly with your servant, my lord?"

"Not this time, Razorbill."

"Thank you, my lord."

Mockingbird let a moment pass for Razorbill to process, then he continued, "Perhaps you thought it was I who would captain this ship, but I have decided that you will be at the helm of the Masked Mimic. Eagle has his captain, and I shall have mine."

"I am honored, my lord. If it is your will, I will be the one to personally give the traitor Peregrine what he deserves."

The Major cackled fiendishly, clapped his hands together with sinister delight, and granted Razorbill permission to fulfill his murderous request. He added almost sardonically, "By the way, Captain Razorbill, keep your new weapon. It suits you."
Razorbill thanked the Major with a mixture of gratitude and relief as he was dismissed.

Captain Cardinal studied her.

"Do you think that's a good idea, Captain?" the king asked.

The captain looked at him, then at her again, then at him again. "Yes, let her do it." he confirmed. "They both need it,"

The king was in agreement and suggested, "Lady Bluebird, bring her out momentarily. The captain and I will go out first and prepare Hyla."

"As you wish, Your Majesty," the lady replied.
The king and the captain exited the washroom, finding Hyla still secured defensively above them.

"Hyla," Captain Cardinal said graciously, "I'm very glad to see you're alive."
At the calming sight of him, she reservedly returned her trusty weapon to its resting place, then effortlessly dropped back to the nest-bed.

Grateful that the door had been opened to him, the captain acknowledged her disgruntled feelings and assured her, "You made it possible for me to be here, and I owe my life to you. We all do."

"All of Animystia does," Lord Peacock emphatically agreed.

The captain went on, imploring, "She has forgiven you and wants to tell you so herself, if you'll let her. Will you allow her to, and will you find your way to forgive her yourself?"

Hyla loved Captain Cardinal for the compassionate way he spoke. Her lime green countenance brightened, and she blushed when she realized she was in the favorable presence of the king as well. The door cracked behind him, and Lady Bluebird peaked her head out.

"Bring her out," the benevolent king encouraged.

The lady obliged and opened the door the rest of the way, allowing Saddleback to step out into the view of the tentatively receptive Hyla. The Amphibian saw that the Lepidopteran standing there with twitching wings was truly sorry and, suddenly feeling the same compassion, offered with joyful tears her own sincere apology.

Captain Cardinal studied her.
"Do you think that's a good idea, Captain?" the king asked.

The captain looked at him, then at her again, then at him again. "Yes, let her do it." he confirmed. "They both need it,"

The king was in agreement and suggested, "Lady

Bluebird, bring her out momentarily. The captain and I will go out first and prepare Hyla."

"As you wish, Your Majesty," the lady replied.
The king and the captain exited the washroom, finding Hyla still secured defensively above them.

"Hyla," Captain Cardinal said graciously, "I'm very glad to see you're alive."
At the calming sight of him, she reservedly returned her trusty weapon to its resting place, then effortlessly dropped back to the nest-bed.

Grateful that the door had been opened to him, the captain acknowledged her disgruntled feelings and assured her, "You made it possible for me to be here, and I owe my life to you. We all do."

"All of Animystia does," Lord Peacock emphatically agreed.

The captain went on, imploring, "She has forgiven you and wants to tell you so herself, if you'll let her. Will you allow her to, and will you find your way to forgive her yourself?"

Hyla loved Captain Cardinal for the compassionate way he spoke. Her lime green countenance brightened, and she blushed when she realized she was in the favorable presence of the king as well. The door cracked behind him, and Lady Bluebird peaked her head out.

"Bring her out," the benevolent king encouraged.

The lady obliged and opened the door the rest of the way, allowing Saddleback to step out into the view of the tentatively receptive Hyla. The Amphibian saw that

the Lepidopteran standing there with twitching wings
was truly sorry and, suddenly feeling the same compassion, offered with joyful tears her own sincere apology.

Chapter XII - Forgiveness

Peregrine, meanwhile, had been exercising his newly grafted and now functional attributes. Captain Blue Jay had been successful in adapting his new ally's physiology with the cybernetic wing enhancements, and the bullet-fast Avian was shredding the sky around the Cobalt Cloud. Try as he might, the ship's captain could barely keep tabs on Peregrine's lightning trajectory.

"Wow," Captain Blue Jay breathed in astonishment when Peregrine was finished, "that blasted 'Major' of yours isn't going to know what hit him."

"What is our next course of action?" Peregrine asked.

"We are en route to rendezvous with King Eagle and his companions. We'll be joi—"

"Oh, no," Peregrine said, cutting the other short, "I am on board with you, Captain, but I'm done with him."

Perplexed, Captain Blue Jay responded, "I thought Mockingbird was the enemy?"

"Look, you don't know what happened," Peregrine said bitterly. "I don't want to see him, and he wouldn't want to see me either. Anyway, I can take out Mockingbird all by myself."

The astute captain knew he was making excuses and pleaded, "Peregrine, come on. I understand something happened between you two, but you can't do this on your own, and we can't do this without him. Tell you what, you can stay on the ship when we get there, and he doesn't even need to know you are with us."

"Fine, as long as I don't have to see him, and I get to gut Mockingbird myself—"

"Great," the clever captain said, gently cutting him off. Proceeding to usher him out, he suggested, "Why don't you go catch up with Canary?"

Peregrine left the captain's cabin, shaking his head. He closed the door and, as soon as he turned around, Canary ran up to him.

"Come with me, Peregrine," she said, taking his hand and leading him to her cabin. Once they were alone, she began by saying, "I want you to know what happened to me after the siege and how I came to be part of Captain Blue Jay's crew. I admit, I admired you, and when I saw you side with Mockingbird, I didn't know what to think, so I flew. I flew until I found Captain Blue Jay. I felt safe with him, and he offered me a place on his crew. I can't say I haven't suffered feelings of guilt over the forfeiture of my designation though."

"I understand," he empathized.

"What happened to your wings?" she asked delicately.

"Mockingbird did," he said bitterly.

"Oh, Peregrine, I'm sorry."

"Don't be. He'll get what's coming to him, thanks to this upgrade from Captain Blue Jay."

She ran her fingers down a metallic edge and admitted, "Captain Blue Jay really is wonderful," then added with an undertone of jealousy, "Tryxie is lucky."

"Then why are you willing to allow him to join forces with Eagle?" he retorted.

She thought for a moment before answering him. "It's a little more complicated than that, Peregrine" she said. Blue Jay and Eagle are actually apparently very close. Blue Jay does his own thing, never wanting to be a 'Lord' or sit at the table where we both had a place, though Eagle always thought a seat belonged to him. Anyway, Captain Blue Jay was often called upon to serve our kingdom in less overt ways, and he never failed to oblige. I'm not angry with Eagle. I used to be, but I've forgiven him."

"I'm not sure I can," Peregrine said, "and I know I can't forgive Mockingbird."

She took his hand, tenderly this time, looked him in the eye with compassion, and said, "You will find your way, Peregrine. Don't be afraid."
He couldn't handle her kindness, so he stood abruptly, and left her alone in her cabin.

———————————

At Cloud Castle, the residents were gathered together on the deck of the Crimson Crest, which stood magnificently on its custom platform. Captain Cardinal took position at the helm, facing his crew. Sir Albatross stood at his right.

"All of you know the mission," the captain began.

"We're taking the fight to Mockingbird on his own turf. We're going to Bedim to infiltrate our enemy's base in order to rescue our queen and Rosy's dear brother. There will certainly be challenges, but I understand Rosy has set things up to greatly enhance our chances of getting the captives out unnoticed. Some of us might have to engage in battle, but that will be merely a distraction, while others will be led by Rosy through a secret tunnel to where our queen and Brambling are being held. I believe we're expected to have additional help as well."

Initially, the mood was uncertain, but Sir Albatross backed him up, exhorting, "Friends, brothers and sisters, don't be timid. We have Captain Cardinal, and Phoenix Prime is indeed with us. We can't lose. We are assured victory."

His gentle and firm tone was persuasive, but there was still some collective hesitancy. Lord Peacock, sensing this and taking courage, stepped up beside his fellow lord as a statement that he stood with them.

"Thank you, my friends," said the captain to the two lords.

Sir Albatross was doing his duty, which he always did well. Lord Peacock really wasn't concerned about rescuing Brambling, but he knew the crew had to be united under the captain's leadership for the sake of the queen. Feelings toward her were unanimous among her kinsmen. She was loved and admired, and they sincerely desired to see her back at their king's side, whatever the cost. How each one felt about Brambling varied, but there were no real grievances toward him. Rosy and Starling had both spent much time praying for him.

Forgiveness had been a practice instilled in all those who valued the king's wisdom. At meals and on other occasions, he would demonstrate by praying with them for the likes of Brambling, Peregrine, and even Mockingbird. There was a full expectation by the juveniles that Brambling would be reunited with them completely transformed in his spirit, even as Saddleback was both inwardly and outwardly. Rosy, in particular, had been envisioning herself and Starling together in the favor and blessing of her brother.

The collected company was filled with inspiration, and King Eagle arrived just in time to see them off. Perceiving the great grace that was upon them, he pronounced, "My beloved children, I am immensely proud of each of you. No force on Animystia can hope to defeat you, for you are united as one. Furthermore, Phoenix Prime is with us and is giving us additional assistance. Our beloved Captain Blue Jay and his crew are en route to rendezvous with us here."

Chapter XIII –
Captains, Compliments, And Condolences

As King Eagle finished briefing his subjects about their imminent company, a patch of white slowly drifted by. By the time anyone realized it was as close as it actually was, it began to roll away, revealing the presence of their anticipated arrivals. Merlin had repaired the damaged engine of the Cobalt Cloud's Cloud Generator, though he himself was not presently aboard the cloudship. Its unveiling was awesome to behold, and a smiling waving crew greeted the others warmly.

The guest vessel put down beside the Crimson Crest, and the contrast was striking. Those who were on board disembarked and began making introductions or being reunited. The king introduced the two captains to one another, and they firmly shook hands.

"Captain Cardinal, I've heard a great deal about you," Captain Blue Jay heartily expressed. "I'm looking forward to this adventure together."

"Thank you, Captain Blue Jay, the crimson captain remarked. "I'm looking forward to it as well, and it is an honor to meet you."

"The honor is mine, thank you," the cool-colored captain returned the compliment.

"What's the matter?" the first asked the second, reading his expression.
"I was just thinking, I'm only sorry Captain Quetzal isn't running the skies anymore."

"Captain Quetzal?" the king inquired. "Do we know what happened to him?"

"I'm not entirely sure, but I heard much of his crew perished in an altercation in the Western Realm, and the whereabouts of the Emerald Egg remain unknown to us."

"I sense he's actually still alive," Captain Cardinal said. "I'm seeing a figure that seems to be him, but he looks quite odd, and I'm hearing the name, 'Green Hermit.'"

"What's that now?" Captain Blue Jay asked.

"He knows things," the king mused.

Delightfully intrigued, the captain pressed further, "What do you mean?"

"Phoenix Prime is inside of him, and their identities are intertwined in a way," came the attempted explanation, based on the king's own limited understanding.

"Hmm, amazing," Blue Jay concluded, "this is going to take some getting used to."
The three of them chortled cheerfully, then the tone shifted back to serious.

"Did anyone else survive?" the king asked.

"Our Lady Hummingbird and Needletail were the only ones who made it out. As for the rest," Captain Blue Jay lamented, lowering his beak, "I'm sorry, Your Majesty." The brim of his hat cast a forlorn shadow across his face.

"As am I," Captain Cardinal offered.

"My condolences also for your son," Blue Jay added.

"Thank you, my friends," said the king. "We shall have a memorial in all their honor when this is ordeal is over with. It's time for you to depart. Are you ready?"

"We are," the captains replied in unison.

"Then call your companies, and let us pray," the king instructed.

With two successive summoning cries, the entire assembly was quickly before the king. He gathered them around in a circle and began lifting up his voice in acknowledgment and thanksgiving to Phoenix Prime for their victory and the safe return of each of them and the loved ones they were going to rescue, then gave Captain Cardinal the floor.

Beginning with Sir Albatross on his right and ending with the king on his left, the chosen hero spoke words of encouragement, exhortation, and comfort to each of them. Afterward, there was a general atmosphere of edification. This ennobling interchange helped to forge an even stronger unity and love for one another, and a peace covered the whole assembly that transcended any normal reasoning.

As the pair of complimentary ships departed, King Eagle looked on with pride through tears of joy. He watched the two captains as they stood facing each other, saluting from their respective vessels. The blue and red dots receded, appearing like drops of water and blood, and he flew to his solar to meditate.

While the heroes on Volar were strengthened by blessing, Major Mockingbird was "motivating" his own forces. The crew of the Masked Mimic was preparing to launch its own attack against their incoming visitors, and it delighted the Major to have received the knowledge through his spy agency that they would not have to make the assault on Cloud Castle directly this time. Razorbill stood on his right, and the stench of cruelty emanated from both of them.

Crossbill and eight others had been sitting around two fairly large wooden tables in the dining hall of Mockingbird's Nest, each having his or her fill of Mr. Mallard's finest brewed beverage. A case had been left on board the Masked Mimic for them as an added gesture of good form to the deal. Bishop and Kestrel were absent, but their presences were hardly missed, and Mockingbird was not concerned with squandering precious resources on what he considered worthless pursuits. The names of the eight were Rook, Thrush, Shrike, Oriola, Dragonfly, Skylark, Vultura (who was also in Jack's dream), and Robinette (to whom the unexpectantly vacant throne belonged). Their revelry had been disrupted upon the arrival of Major Mockingbird and his new captain, and there was nearly an uproar when Rook's glass was shattered, but it quickly died when they beheld the smoking gun in the Major's hand.

"The time has come," Mockingbird decreed, "and it couldn't be more perfect. Captain Cardinal has only just arrived here, despite Peregrine's pitiful efforts, and we have every means necessary to destroy him. We're going to take care of Eagle and their entire cursed flock once and for all. Not only do we have the guns, but now we have the Masked Mimic, and they will never see us coming." He cackled fiendishly as Razorbill emptied a bag of holstered firearms on one of the tables.

"Hear, hear," they shouted, raising their glasses. The drunken Rook's only had its bottom left, and his last few sips splashed out unnoticed.

Whereas King Eagle's allies were united in love and faith, the gruesome things uniting these dark souls were their fear, hatred, and pride. The reasons for each of their twisted and morbid hearts varied, some even now despising Razorbill for his promotion. Except for one, however, they all had a common interest in seeing the downfall of the King of the Northern Realm.

———

Meanwhile, Brambling and Queen Barbary were earnestly praying in the equally grim confines below. The queen had an indescribable joy that Phoenix Prime had put in her heart, and her faith was so strong that it even surprised her. She couldn't understand why, but she just had a certainty that help was presently on its way, and she thanked the Spirit with all her heart for their imminent rescue. To further her delight, she heard Brambling praying with gratitude for a positive reunion with his sister and for reconciliation with Starling.

The mostly intoxicated miscreants above were each greedily selecting firearms for themselves, completely thoughtless of the prisoners. They had all watched demonstrations of how to use them by Mockingbird and Razorbill. Some of them were pretty astute and probably could have figured it out themselves anyway. Not all of them were that savvy, though, and a gunshot ricocheting from the fortified ceiling almost hit Skylark.

Jumping and squawking in terror, he demanded, "What's the big idea?" Glaring at Thrush, who had unintentionally pulled the trigger, he was ready to fire his own weapon.

The others began laughing heartily at his expense, though, and before there could be any further reaction, Razorbill screeched to grab their attention. Though the new captain wasn't much respected overall by them, they all knew that if they crossed him, they were crossing Major Mockingbird.

"Are you all ready, then?" Razorbill's question sounded more like a command.

"You got lucky," Skylark spat at Thrush as they followed him out.

Subsequently, Captain Razorbill pompously led them to the underground hangar where the Masked Mimic was stationed and, as they began to board, Major

Mockingbird called him aside to sternly admonish him.

"Captain Razorbill, I see no reason why you should be defeated. We have the advantage in every way. We have the weaponry, the numbers, the ship, and we have the power of Dragonyx. But remember, if you fail, you have not only failed me, you have failed him. Need I remind you that he is less tolerant of failure than even I am."

"Understood, my lord." Razorbill grinned sadistically, proud to be in the position granted to him by his master.

Whether or not his captain made it back alive, however, Mockingbird didn't care. He held the same opinion of all his subordinates. Unlike King Eagle, who loved and served his own, this ruler only cared about himself and the evil spirit he served. Like all who are in bondage to evil, though, he did not know that he himself was merely a pawn in a greater manipulation scheme. Once Razorbill got on board, the hangar door opened, shaking the earthen terrain, and the Masked Mimic ascended through the steel-enforced opening. The Crimson Crest and the Cobalt Cloud had left only moments prior, and the gap between the two sides was beginning to close rapidly.

Chapter XIV - Peregrine's Return

Captain Blue Jay had been steadfastly at the helm of the Cobalt Cloud, but presently he felt prompted to go into his cabin and check on Peregrine. When he went in, he found to his disappointment, but not surprise, that his tentative ally had flown the coop. Perturbed, but undistracted, he dismissed the absent speedster and set his face for the mission at hand. He flashed a confident grin at his handsome reflection in the mirror as he doubled back for the door.

He barely had his hand on the handle when a loud crack echoed outside, and he stopped cold. Another went off moments later, and he thought it sounded like the present he had gotten Tryxie from his recent trip to Ambrosia, but he doubted that was it. She herself burst in at that moment, almost knocking him down. Panic-stricken and apologetic, she clutched his vest and buried herself in his chest.

"What is it, love? What's happening?" he asked, wrapping his arms around her to comfort her.

Her response was muffled, but she managed, "They're here, baby."

"Who's here?"

"Mockingbird..."

"Mockingbird's here?"

"His ship…"

"When did he get a ship?"

"We thought it was a passing merchant ship, but

it's them. Oh, baby, it's them!"

"Come on," he said, taking her by the hand. Withdrawing his gun with the other, he exited the cabin with her. As they stepped out onto the deck, he laid his eyes on the chaos of warfare going on around them.

Since the Crimson Crest was ahead of them, its occupants had been first to engage the enemy, and now they were under severe attack. The first shot had taken everyone by surprise and had wounded the brave Sir Albatross in the shoulder. To their detriment, three from the enemy vessel had already come close enough that the injured giant had been able to strike back, using his good arm. He had vaulted skyward and slaughtered all three with one full-range motion of his sword; Shrike, Vultura, and Skylark had simultaneously dropped from the sky. The second blast had backfired on its weapon's own wielder, Crossbill, blowing off half his reddish-orange face.

Captain Blue Jay and Tryxie together bore witness to the third shot, and it was the end of Canary. Furious, Tryxie was quick to retaliate. She aimed her gun at her new friend's murderer and fired a revenge shot. Having gotten a fair bit of practice so far, her aim wasn't terrible, but she did miss her mark. Instead of Thrush, her bullet took the other half of Crossbill's face away, leaving a totally headless corpse behind.

Razorbill stood at the bow of the Masked Mimic, reveling in the carnage before him. Captain Cardinal leaped from his ship to the side of his compatriot, Captain Blue Jay, and the two of them faced the sinister foe.

"Captains Cardinal and Blue Jay" he sneered. "Now I am Captain as well!"

"You are a disgrace," Captain Blue Jay retorted.

"Look around you, fools! We have taken you by surprise, and we have the upper hand. You are utterly defeated."

"So you say," replied Captain Cardinal, undaunted.

A greenish blur suddenly leaped from vessel to vessel, and Hyla's elastic tongue swiped rapidly through the open air. Its spiky attachment landed hard, impaling Razorbill's hand. He lost his grip on his firearm, and shrieked in pain. Hyla leaped up from the bow's underside and flip-kicked the wicked captain, knocking him off his feet.

Before his haunches hit the deck, though, and before anyone saw it coming, a lightning-fast hand appeared and grabbed Hyla's throat. Her tongue made its move, but her weapon bounced futilely from a metallic barrier. As she struggled to breathe, she thought she'd pinged a shield, but as she blacked out, she realized it was actually a wing. Peregrine threw her aside callously, and she collapsed unconscious onto the deck.

"No!" shrieked Lord Peacock, who had been watching with a relived horror from the Crimson Crest. He frantically leaped across and immediately tried to attack Peregrine.

Sir Albatross landed in front of him, halting his advance, and charged him to aid their captains against

Razorbill instead. He was first of all protecting Lord Peacock, knowing that he didn't stand a chance against Peregrine, especially with the latter's obvious upgrade. Secondly, he wanted to face Peregrine himself so that they might resume their prior engagement.

As Lord Peacock moved in to assist against Razorbill, he realized the good captains had each already departed to aid others of their company, and he found himself alone against the fiendish but weakened opponent. "You can do this," he told himself confidently, "Phoenix Prime is with you."

Sir Albatross faced Peregrine and cordially expressed to his former ally that he was impressed with the latter's new hardware. Peregrine thanked him and made no immediate attempt to attack him, despite knowing he could have destroyed him easily, given both his technological advantage and his opponent's unfortunate battle damage. Sir Albatross knew it, too, and he sensed that something was going on in the mind of his former friend. Therefore, he did not attempt to strike Peregrine either.

Razorbill, having lost another weapon, was backing away cautiously from Lord Peacock. Despite having sword drawn and ready, the latter considered it bad form to slaughter an unarmed opponent, no matter how clearly deserving. He snatched up a sword from a fallen adversary with his talons and kicked it toward his foe, who managed to catch it in an unexpectedly spectacular fashion.

"Big mistake," Razorbill goaded.

He had become pretty skilled with the gun already, but was deadly with a blade, and made the first move. Countering, Lord Peacock was also a master swordsman and would easily hold his own as the fight turned into a frustrating stalemate.

On the Cobalt Cloud, meanwhile, vain attempts were being made by Tryxie to activate the Cloud Generator. She was unskilled in the process and wished Merlin were there to make it work. He had shown her how to run it before, but she'd never quite gotten the hang of it. All of a sudden, she remembered a little poetic tune Captain Blue Jay had come up with for her to remember in times like these. She began to sing:

> *If wisdom is what you seek*
> *Phoenix Prime gives it to you free*
> *Ask in faith, or you won't receive*
> *Do not doubt, only just believe*

The echoed words of her husband aloud encouraged her, and she began to do them in earnest. Within moments, it became crystal clear to her how to operate the generator, and she put it to work at once. Elated, she rushed back to the deck to find her love before the cover of white engulfed the ship.

Silvereye and Goldeneye, twins on the crew of the

Cobalt Cloud, had been battling Dragonfly and Oriola. As the obscuring screen enveloped their vessel, the twins retreated into the safe haven, having both nearly been shot out of the sky. Although Captain Blue Jay could have supplied them with guns as well, they didn't care for them, so they had chosen not to use them. They swore to each other that they would take better advantage of the technology available to them from that point on.

Lady Bluebird had been defending against Rook and Thrush, alongside Captain Blue Jay, who had joined her when he had seen that she was outnumbered. By the time the fog hit, Thrush had been wounded in his mid-section, and the lady's arm had been scratched by a bullet, which only spurred her on. Rook and Thrush soared into the air and out of the dense smoke-like substance, joining up with Dragonfly and Oriola. The four confused adversaries hovered, tentatively plotting their next move.

Aboard the Crimson Crest, Starling and Rosy were hiding behind some cargo boxes when Robinette spotted them. She drew her gun, but when she realized who they were, she quickly holstered it. They were nevertheless on the defensive, and Starling had his hand on his knife, ready to do whatever necessary.

"Don't be afraid," she assured them, "I'm not going to hurt you."

"But you are an enemy, aren't you?" Rosy demanded.

"Not to you," she countered. "I am only after Captain Cardinal."

"You found him," came a definitive voice from behind her.

Startled, she turned around, the tip of her beak at the point of his blade. "Captain," she acknowledged with sincerity.

"What do you want with me?" he inquired, staying his weapon.

She hesitated before answering, then replied, "I know what you have to do, and I have to stop you."

"I'm afraid I don't know what you're talking about," the captain pressed.

"You're going to kill Major Mockingbird, and I can't let you do that."

There was something about the way she said it that made him think she was more than just one of his puppets. He waited, giving her time to explain.

She continued, "I was once in love with him. There was a time when he was good and was called Lord Mockingbird—"

"Good?" Starling squabbled.

"Go on," Captain Cardinal entreated, hushing the juvenile with a polite gesture. Because of Carnelian's memories, the captain actually did know what Robinette was talking about, but he was disposed to have her tell him anyway.

"Yes," she went on, "he was a member of your

king's council, and so was I. When Mockingbird left, I stayed for a little while, but I ended up leaving, too, because I thought I loved him."

"I see," said Captain Cardinal.

"I am not in love with Mockingbird anymore," she continued, "but I can't leave him, or he will surely kill me. He has lost his goodness, but..." She looked away, lamenting.

"Let us take care of him, and let us protect you." She looked at the captain again. "Please don't kill him." she pleaded.

"I assure you, Robinette, killing him is not our first option. Our goal would be to get him to surrender peacefully and return him to Volar to face King Eagle."

"Please," she begged again.

"He may not give us a choice."

"We have a child," she squealed and started bawling.

He was beginning to feel pity for her, but before he could respond, four winged assailants descended and flanked them. Dragonfly, Oriola, Rook, and Thrush began to move in before an unexpected event took them all by surprise.

In response to a vision given by Phoenix Prime, Captain Cardinal discovered a wave of fire spreading throughout his entire being. He knew that it was the Spirit of Phoenix Prime at work, and he let the personality take over. His eyes blazed like the sun, and his sword began to glow like coals in a fire. "Separate us with a hedge of protection," he cried, and a wall of flame suddenly encircled him, along with Starling and Rosy.

The fire did not consume the three, but the wrath of its heat was sorely felt by their enemies, and Dragonfly permanently fainted. Peregrine witnessed the spectacular event from the enemy ship and, in that moment, believed in the possible reality of the prophecy concerning Captain Cardinal for the first time. He passed a sly look across the length of two swords, and Sir Albatross caught his meaning. Peregrine was about to do what he had really come there to do.

He glanced with a tinge of remorse at the unconscious Hyla laying on the deck. He hadn't desired to hurt her, but he had done what he had done to her in order that he might win Razorbill's trust before destroying him. The double agent and Sir Albatross began to move closer to where Lord Peacock and Razorbill were fighting.

Lord Peacock had been disarmed, pinned down, and he was about to be dispatched. Razorbill was taunting and mocking him, but the lord was undaunted by his adversary's cruel words. He was ready to die honorably, but fortunately for him, he wasn't going to have to at this time. Peregrine turned away from Sir Albatross and, with one swift motion of a razor-sharp wing, cleanly severed Razorbill's own means of flight. In pain and anger, the enemy whirled around to strike, and his attack hand was sliced off by Peregrine's other wing.

Chapter XV - The Dome

With the captain of the Masked Mimic and several of its crew apparently dead and/or missing, including Robinette having been taken captive, the ship's remaining crew attempted a hasty retreat. Having knowledge through observation of how to fly the ship, Thrush had taken it upon himself to guide it back to their base on Bedim, despite his injury. Given their situation, none of them looked forward to approaching Major Mockingbird, but they would make it back or die trying.

The Crimson Crest and the Cobalt Cloud pursued the Masked Mimic to the dark island and watched uneasily as the enemy ship disappeared into the underground hangar. Its steel jaws closed, and large spikes covered the platform, making it unsuitable to land on. Captain Cardinal signaled to Captain Blue Jay that they would have to keep their ships afloat and anchor them to the outer trees. Once the ships were both secure, Captain Cardinal gathered the entire team together on his ship and began to lay out their strategy, addressing Rosy first.

"Yes, Captain Cardinal," she acknowledged, saluting with gusto.

He smiled at her zeal and sincerity. "Since you know where the queen and your brother are being held, take Starling and Tryxie with you to free them, then return here immediately."

"Yes, Sir," she replied, saluting again, beaming with admiration.

"Sir Albatross," the crimson captain addressed, "let me restore your wound, as I did King Eagle's."

"Captain Cardinal," he said humbly, "my gratitude."

The captain did as before; removing his glove, he stretched his hand out to the gentle giant's shoulder. Utterance indiscernible to the natural mind resonated from the former's vocal cords. The wound was supernaturally undone in the presence of them all as the bullet dislodged itself. This sign of authority concerning the subject of prophecy caused quite a stir to arise from the few souls present who were less or altogether unfamiliar with it. Captain Blue Jay did well with settling his compatriots, giving them faith in the illustrious hero. With gratitude, Captain Cardinal gave the honor to Phoenix Prime.
To his first mate, he advised, "Sir Albatross, I know you're more than capable of fighting, but we have enough muscle for what I hope will be mostly a stealth mission, and I also need you to keep a watchful eye on our guest, Lady Robinette. If you'd be so kind, please stay with her and our ships."

"Very well, Captain."

"Thank you, my friend. We'll see you upon our return."

Sir Albatross bowed his head, extended his right hand, and said, "Phoenix Prime be with you."

The captain completed a firm handshake. "Phoenix Prime be with you."

The noble lord took his leave and went below

deck.

"Captain Blue Jay," Captain Cardinal continued, "you and I will find Mockingbird and detain him."

"By Phoenix Prime," his fellow captain declared. "Peregrine, you take the rest, and provide a distraction if his henchmen attack us—"

"Captain," Peregrine interjected, "let me come with you. This is personal."

"Peregrine," Captain Cardinal replied, "I know what you want to do, but I cannot allow it, at least not yet. For one thing, he must stand before our king. Secondly, he and Robinette have a son."

"Your king, Captain. I may believe that you might be what the prophesy says, but   I'm still not allegiant to Eagle, and what's this joke about a son? Mockingbird and Robinette don't have a son."

"I don't believe she was lying when she told me."

"I've never seen him," Peregrine flatly stated. "With all due respect, Captain, I think you have been lied to."

Captain Cardinal sighed and conceded, "Very well, Peregrine. You come with me, but do not harm Mockingbird. We will take him before the king, and King Eagle will decide his fate."

"Captain," he said sharply.

"Peregrine, I don't pretend to understand what he did to you, but revenge isn't going to heal the wound. I need you, if you are to come with me, to be focused and not blinded by emotion."

"Fine."

"That's the spirit," Captain Blue Jay interjected. "Listen, I know how you feel about Eagle. It's not going to be easy, but you can do it. Forget the king. Trust in Phoenix Prime."

Captain Cardinal expressed his gratitude to his fellow captain and asked him, "Will you lead the others and provide our cover?"

"You got it, Captain," he replied.

Captain Cardinal looked at each of them in turn. "Rosy," he inquired, "are you ready?"

"Yes, Sir," she confirmed.

"Captain Blue Jay?"

"Indeed, I am," he acknowledged.

"Peregrine?"

"Let's just do this," he said, shaking his head.

"Very well," Captain Cardinal concluded, then pronounced, "Phoenix Prime be with us all."

With several amens, Rosy and the other two members of her trio took off. Captain Cardinal shook Captain Blue Jay's hand and sent the latter off with his team. Extending a hand to Peregrine for one last vote of confidence, the crimson captain appealed with all sincerity, "Peregrine, I need you."

Briefly hesitating before accepting his hand, Peregrine petitioned, "Captain?"

"Yes, Peregrine?"

"If I can't kill him, can I at least injure him badly?"

Captain Cardinal laughed, shook his head, and

said, "Come on, Peregrine, let's go get him."

"Alright," Peregrine consented, and Captain Cardinal saw him smile for the first time. "We may have a problem, though," Peregrine stated, and the pleasant expression vanished.

"What's that?"

"There are only two entrances I know of besides Rosy's, and both are going to be difficult to penetrate."

"I see," said the captain, "where are the entrances?"

"The fortress is a mostly covered dome, and the main point of entry is in the middle of the front, but it'll be locked. The other is through the underground hangar, which is obviously closed and fortified."

"Ideas?"

"Mockingbird's throne room is on the top level. Maybe there's a way in up there I don't know about… or maybe we can make one," Peregrine suggested.

"I trust you," the captain affirmed. "Take us there."

"Thanks," Peregrine acknowledged appreciatively. Even if he didn't fully realize it, he was glad he could be found trustworthy. To his surprise, he found himself able to trust as well.

The top of the dome fortress was covered almost entirely with masses of vines, like thick cables, and dense foliage. They hovered, pondering their course of action, agreeing that swords and probably even Peregrine's new sharp and powerful wings weren't going to do much good.

"Captain?" he suggested, coming up with an idea.

.   "What is it, Peregrine?"

"I didn't have any faith in the prophecy concerning you. I'm still not quite fully convinced of everything, but I saw what you did on the ship with the fire."

"Peregrine, that wasn't me," Captain Cardinal replied. "Phoenix Prime did that through me, and I didn't make it happen."

"But you do seem to have a connection with Phoenix Prime that no one else ever has," he admitted. "Can you pray or something?"

"You're right, Peregrine," the captain confirmed. "I will pray." He looked up and gave thanks to Phoenix Prime, and immediately he felt the power coursing through him. His eyes kindled, and his blade began to glow again. He gripped the tangle with his talons and, twirling his sword, he struck downward. Searing through ropes of heavy vines, its scalding tip penetrated the dome's steely surface. The foliage burned to ash, and the substance of the wall began to melt like butter. He proceeded to scorch a hole large enough for each of them to fit through, and once they had both given their gratitude to Phoenix Prime, they slipped through the breach.

CHAPTER XVI - THE RUBY EDGE

The top level of the dome was split in half by a wall, and Mockingbird's throne was on one side of it. Captain Cardinal and Peregrine had come in just on the other, in front of an imposing steely door, which was engraved with strange cryptic markings. The captain carefully attempted to open the door but, unsurprisingly, it was locked. He looked at Peregrine, who looked undeterred.

"Got it covered," Peregrine whispered. Revealing a skeleton key, he almost imperceptibly unlocked the door, impressing the captain. They both considered that Major Mockingbird himself might be just on the other side of the door, but they shared a feeling of doubt, given the disturbingly evident silence. Nevertheless, Peregrine wisely exercised caution while cracking open the door. A bullet ricocheted just above his hand, and he immediately extracted his still intact appendage, backing away quietly from the door.

Captain Cardinal motioned to his ally what he had in mind, and the latter nodded that he understood. Peregrine kicked in the door and darted back behind the wall as the daring captain made his move. The latter dove into the throne room diagonally and went into a roll, releasing a sharp projectile. Before the target had time to react, the hero's dagger had impaled his gun hand, causing him to screech and drop the weapon. Rebounding off the steely floor, the gun fired again, and its bullet hit a backwards throne. Curious, the captain wondered to himself why it was turned around, and he beckoned his partner.

Peregrine had heard the gun shot and was hesitant to go in, afraid the captain might have failed. When he heard his name, however, he dashed into the room, ready for action.

The young figure with the bloody hand immediately took him by surprise, for it clearly wasn't Mockingbird. Malevolence and disdain were not in the eyes staring back at him, just a general bitterness, and there was no recognition of one by the other.

Though the Avian in question was vulnerable and frightened, Peregrine still considered him a threat. He would have clipped by him in an instant, but the room wasn't exceptionally large, and even the aerial speedster's lowest velocity required a much more open space. Rather than risk slamming into a wall, he gauged his next move by Captain Cardinal.

The captain was watching carefully as their enemy painfully removed the dagger, clenching it with his good hand. Taking the nod, Peregrine was about to move in, but he barely took a step before a desperate scream interrupted him. Robinette came seemingly out of nowhere, and threw herself in between them, attempting to protect the young and frightened individual.

"Robinette!" the captain and Peregrine simultaneously proclaimed.

"Don't hurt him!" she pleaded.

Wondering what had become of his first mate, the truth of the matter became clear to the captain, and he addressed his comrade, "Peregrine, listen to her. This is her son."

"What?" Peregrine retorted. He was already angry, and he thought he might have been hearing things. After the initial shock of disbelief wore off, though, he understood himself. He was about to say something else, but he was unable to open his beak before a long, pointed, reddish object stuck out in front of his face. It was the blade of a peculiar sword, and it had been viciously run through both Robinette and her son, binding them together.

When the instrument of death was withdrawn, and the two victims had fallen lifeless to the floor, a figure immediately identifiable to Peregrine stood visible. While the intruders had been distracted, Major Mockingbird's throne had been silently rotating on its platform. He had been waiting for an opportune time to reveal himself, and now that he had done so, the question of why the throne had been turned around had been answered. Livid, Peregrine swooped back next to the captain.

"I've been expecting you, Captain Cardinal," the Major sneered.

"Here I am," the captain replied boldly.

"And Peregrine, what a displeasure to see you again, alive and well."

"No thanks to you," Peregrine spat.

"How did you get those?" the Major mocked, indicating the technologically enhanced wings. "Did you swindle the Duck?"

Vengeance swallowed Peregrine, and he drew his sword. "Mockingbird, you fool. You've just slaughtered your only protection. Now, I'm going to kill you," he proclaimed.

Captain Cardinal moved to retrieve his dagger from the grip of Mockingbird's dead son, all the while keeping a keen eye on the lethal instrument in the Major's possession. He had understandably thought at first that its blade was the same hue as his crimson feathers because of the blood of its victims, but he clearly saw now that its ruby coloration was natural. Mentally, he revisited the wardrobe in his quarters on the Crimson Crest, and he recalled the empty stand, which read "The Ruby Edge."

Peregrine attacked, and Major Mockingbird deflected his blow. He struck again, and his strike was parried again. He slashed a third time, and it was also no match for the enemy's defense. It seemed as if the rosy blade was actually moving on its own accord to where it perceived the edge of his own would land. The master swordsman's frustration was mounting because he knew he was certainly a much better duelist than Mockingbird, and he was sure it would have been over quickly. "It has to be the sword," he thought.

It was apparent to both him and Captain Cardinal that the only way they were going to prevail would be to remove the unusual sword from the Major's grasp, though how do so presented a challenge. The captain did not wish to dishonor Peregrine by attempting to aid him, but he knew his partner could not find an opening on his own; the blade was too accurate. As he considered his options, he surrendered to the Spirit within him. Falling into a trance, he was flooded with revelation about the sword. He knew it belonged to him, and he understood its desire to be wielded by him. Holding out his right hand, he uttered something unintelligible as a holy fire blazed in his eyes. Immediately, the Ruby Edge began to heat up, and fire emanated from its blade. Mockingbird compulsively dropped the scalding sword, but it vanished before it hit the floor and reappeared, back to normal, in the captain's hand.

Peregrine made his move and, in a matter of seconds, both he and Mockingbird had disappeared. The vengeful Avian had bound the Major with a lightweight detainment cord, and before Captain Cardinal could stop him, he had flown the coop, carrying his prey with him through the hole in which he and the captain had entered. The captain was tempted to think he'd made the wrong choice by allowing Peregrine to come, but the knowledge that he was now needed elsewhere drove away the inclination to ponder potential failure.

Chapter XVII - Black And Blue

Captain Blue Jay had done his job successfully. He and his companions had provided an adequate distraction to deter the remaining minions of Major Mockingbird from noticing Starling, Rosy, and Tryxie as the three slipped into the trapdoor Rosy had discovered at the edge of the stronghold's backside. The opening led straight into the dungeon below Mockingbird's Nest, whose layout she knew fairly well, given her short time there. Once they had entered the dim underground passageway, she led them straight to their captive friends.

Initially, upon their reunion, a slight tension arose between Starling and Brambling because neither knew what to expect from the other. This quickly dissolved, however, as Brambling offered Starling a genuine apology. The latter forgave him, as he had already decided to in his heart. Rosy was overjoyed that she didn't have to bear divisive hearts between the two because she loved them both very much.

Though she was thrilled, the reality of the present situation kicked back in, and she immediately reached for the lockpick she had tucked away in a pouch. She opened the steely cage doors to her brother's cell and, with Starling's help, swiftly brought him out. Tryxie aided Queen Barbary and, once they were free, Rosy fearlessly led the way back out.

The moment she opened the trapdoor, however, a jet-black hand grabbed her from the other side and pulled her through. Starling was right behind her, and by the time he had realized what was happening, she was gone. He screamed and tried to get out to rescue her, but the trapdoor had been shut, and something was putting weight on top of it. He frantically strained against it, but to no avail, and the passageway was too narrow for a collective effort.

The blade of a sword suddenly penetrated the patch from above, nearly impaling Starling, whose own life was of no importance to him at that moment. He could hear the one he loved screaming, and the agony drove him to push even harder as he cried out her name. Above ground, the owner of the black hand was clutching the throat of his victim with it. From head to toe, this malevolent being was black as night. Even his eyes were a dark abyss. Rosy's screaming abruptly ceased, and helplessness enshrouded Starling, who was still trapped below.

Brambling was petrified with horror, but Tryxie was furious. She forced Starling and Brambling out of the way, got into position underneath the dark adversary, and drew her gun. She had intended to shoot him through the trapdoor, but when she cocked the hammer, he recognized it, and immediately removed himself from the line of fire. After she pulled the trigger, she heard what sounded like a body dropping. Peeking through the hole in the opening, she saw nothing, so she decided to test the door. It gave way, and she considered that she had eliminated their foe. She made her way out and stood up, but the only body on the ground was Rosy's. A moment later, she heard the sound of another gun being cocked behind her head. Another identical sound behind that replaced the second of terror she felt.

Captain Blue Jay had gotten the drop on the cold adversary, and stated triumphantly, "Found you, Rook."

"Captain Blue Jay," his target acknowledged, and a slight grin spread across his wicked beak.

"Thought you had me fooled, did you?" the capricious captain heckled.

"You are a sly one."

"And you, Rook, are a dead one."

"Shoot me, and she dies," the enemy threatened.

Starling, Brambling, and Queen Barbary had all climbed out, but none of them were in a position to help. Starling was paralyzed at seeing Rosy crumpled on the ground, and Brambling and the queen were still somewhat weak and stiff from their cramped imprisonment. Tensions were mounting, and a decision was going to have to be made from one side or the other.

Suddenly, a flash of ruby cut off the barrel of Rook's firearm, leaving him vulnerable and at the mercy of Captain Blue Jay. A friendly figure landed next to him, and one captain was glad to see the other. Captain Cardinal had arrived just in time, and his compatriot relished the turn of events. Blue Jay holstered his gun and drew his blade as Rook spun around to face him. The adumbral assailant attempted to slash him, but the swift captain caught his arm, stopping his attack. Locking eyes, the latter ran his steel straight through the former's black heart. Still breathing, the vicious villain began spewing curses at the unmoved captain, who was staring him down with somber finality. Changing the hand holding the hilt of his sword, Captain Blue Jay slyly redrew his firearm with the other. He pressed the hole of its barrel against Rook's temple, and pulled the trigger. Deftly removing his sword from the corpse's chest cavity, he carelessly allowed the body to fall. The cool captain blew the smoke off the barrel, whirled the lethal weapon around his finger, and replaced it in its holster. Afterward, he knelt down and wiped his sword off on Rook's tunic, before sliding it back into its sheath.

Captain Cardinal rebuked Captain Blue Jay with a look for taking delight in his kill, then quickly explained to him what had happened to Peregrine and Major Mockingbird. He urgently suggested, "We need to get the others and get out of here now."

"Of course," Captain Blue Jay replied, humbled. Seeing the hurting juveniles, he asked Starling, "is Rosy alive?"

"Yes," the young Avian sobbed, grateful she wasn't dead.

Captain Cardinal solemnly thanked Phoenix Prime himself and asked Tryxie to escort them, along with Brambling and Queen Barbary, to the Cobalt Cloud. The captains then both took off, soaring past trees and rocks, coming to the area around the hangar where the rest of their allies were still engaged in battle. They saw Goldeneye and Silvereye forced back-to-back, with Thrush and Oriola closing in from either side. Though the twins were fighting fiercely, the villains were keeping them at bay. "Use your gun," Thrush yelled at Oriola, having lost his.

"Oh, right!" Trading hands with her sword, she drew her firearm.

Moments later, Silvereye's light-grey breast feathers were soaked in dark red. Her twin was terror struck, and Thrush took advantage of the fateful distraction. He kneed Goldeneye in the chest, followed by an uppercut with the hilt of his sword, cracking the latter's skull.

As the pair of captains drew close, a certain Lepidopteran descended over the carnage, fluttering angrily. In Saddleback's new phase, her antagonism was toward one of the remaining foes, and the air was thick around Thrush with her poisonous pheromones. Oriola tried to use her gun again, but before she even had it cocked, a sharp metallic instrument hit her square in the neck, dropping her instantly. Thrush bolted after Hyla, who leaped out of harm's way. Subsequently, he crashed dead out of the air and landed hard on the ground, leaving a bloody trail. Saddleback and Hyla shared a triumphant gesture from a safe distance, celebrating their teamwork as a sign of peace between them.

With no enemies left, and heavy hearts remaining, Captain Cardinal's mind wandered back to his departed ally and the threat the latter had carried off to unknown consequences. Others began to wonder about Peregrine and Mockingbird as well. The captain was beginning to attempt an explanation, but was interrupted.

"Don't bother," came a voice from nearby, just beyond the edge of the island. Peregrine himself was hovering there. He was holding a lacerated, eviscerated, and decapitated Major Mockingbird. "There is nothing major about this worthless counterfeit." he declared.

There was a chilling tension amongst the onlookers.

"Pride always comes before the fall," he said mockingly to his kill, and he spitefully dropped the lifeless body of the failed tyrant into oblivion.

Captain Cardinal lamented this outcome, and Peregrine zipped off with no explanation, still erroneously believing that he was the only one he was really accountable to.

Chapter XVIII – The King

Starling and Brambling were invited to stay in their cabin and look after Rosy for the ride. Brambling, the once overprotective older brother, now saw how much Starling truly cared about his sister, and he was now at peace with and even supportive of their relationship. Brambling's approval really mattered to Rosy, but her unfortunate condition left her presently unable to revel in a full reunion. For Queen Barbary, Captain Blue Jay and Tryxie made accommodations befitting majesty to the best of their ability.

"I'm so sorry for your losses," the queen consoled them. "I thank you with my whole heart for coming to our rescue and for your hospitality."

"Thank you, Your Majesty," Captain Blue Jay replied. "If you need anything further, let us know. If you'll pardon us, we'll take our leave."

"Of course, thank you, Captain."

Captain Blue Jay and Tryxie retired to their cabin, and he held her in his comforting arms, both of them mourning and weeping.

———

Aboard the Crimson Crest, the truth was revealed regarding an unanswered question. Sir Albatross was found broken down and weeping in a corner of his cabin. "I had to let her go," he sobbed ashamedly when he saw

Captain Cardinal standing concerned in the doorway.

"I understand," the captain replied. He shrewdly opted not to tell the confused Avian lord what had become of Robinette, never mind the rest of her story. Kneeling down, he laid a comforting hand on the gentle giant's shoulder, the one he had healed. "You did what you had to do, and she did what she had to. Whatever you need to forgive yourself of, please do, and know I forgive you also." He spoke to the shame and commanded it to leave.

Sir Albatross began to expel the lying breath, and there was a slight contortion in his watery eyes. As he yawned, new tears of joy began flooding out the tears of sorrow.

"Now, we have to get back, come on," the captain urged, and he offered the redeemed lord his hand, lifting him up.

Lord Peacock and Lady Bluebird had cut the tethers that were binding the ships to the island, and they had excused themselves below. Hyla and Saddleback were given to rest in their own respective places as well. The Amphibian retired to the chest Captain Cardinal had originally found her in, and Saddleback nestled herself into a nook under the hull of the ship, in order to prevent accidentally poisoning the crew.

King Eagle had been residing in his solar, serving

Phoenix Prime with fasting and prayer, while awaiting the company's return. He had been given the ability to see things in the Spirit of Phoenix Prime from the healing and new life the prophetic savior had given him by the Spirit, and he had witnessed much through unseen eyes. However, he was so focused on the vision of his beloved bride returning, he did not foresee the danger coming.

Aboard the Cobalt Cloud, a grave image suddenly flashed in Rosy's mind as she slept, and she remembered something crucially important she hadn't yet revealed to King Eagle. It was difficult enough for her to have shared with him the news that his wife was still alive before, and she had all but buried the knowledge that his son might be as well. She recalled in her dream Prince Heron lying on an operating table in Mockingbird's Nest, and woke up terrified.

"What is it?" Starling and Brambling inquired simultaneously.

"I don't think Prince Heron is dead," she said, shaking.

"Something tells me he's not the only one," Brambling guessed, feeling a strange sensation.

As it turns out, he was right; Razorbill had not perished as everyone supposed. Though he was wounded badly, his wickedness refused to die. Merlin, who had operated as an agent for Mockingbird, though he had no actual fealty to the deceased Major, had discovered Bishop and Kestrel escaping Bedim with the unconscious body of Prince Heron. He had convinced them to bring it to a secret nearby island he was using as an outpost and safehouse. He had an adequate supply of tools and machinery on hand, with which he gave them upgrades, though Heron had already been largely operated on. In addition to armor upgrades, Bishop gained a wrist-mounted flamethrower, and Kestrel an oil gun. Razorbill's body was found and brought there later. His right hand had been replaced by a menacing reaping hook, and he'd been given frightening mechanical substitutes for wings.

————————

Mr. Mallard, the proprietor of the Pekin Duck, among other things, was meanwhile hosting a private audience with an Animystian who had no business being there but was there for business. He was flightless and had fur rather than feathers, paws with claws instead of toes with talons, and incisors and canines in place of a toothless beak.

"Thank you for your services, Lynx," the entrepreneurial Avian concluded with a careful handshake. "Working with Merlin and your supply of technology from the Eastern Realm has been monumental for my profit margins."

"So delighted to be of service, my colleague," the Leonin purred intellectually. "We have just made a discovery that will advance us even further. We will be in touch."

Though it was dawning as the Crimson Crest and the Cobalt Cloud approached the outskirts of Volar, a darkness apart from the passing night remained. The hue of the light beginning to illuminate the sky echoed the moon the night of the mystic transformation. Sir Albatross was keen-eyed at the helm of the Crimson Crest, having the same gut feeling he'd had upon their return through the Rainbow Veil that night, dreading what might be lurking to foil their way home this time. Tryxie stood poised and ready at the wheel of the Cobalt Cloud, sensing herself that something was amiss.

Closing in, Sir Albatross was alarmed to notice two shadowed figures moving violently behind the stained-glass window depicting the prophecy of Captain Cardinal. To his distress, he beheld a cascade of sparkling crimson shards in the wake of a completely helpless King Eagle being thrown forcefully through it. Already severely wounded, the king's wings were shredded by the glass, utterly destroying his ability to fly. Moments before he would have met the ground he ruled over, Bishop and Kestrel revealed themselves to catch the falling majesty, only further crushing the poor Sir Albratross under another unbearable weight of tragic disbelief.

An agonizing call from the multi-vexed Avian summoned the rest of the Avians on the Crimson Crest. Captain Cardinal arrived swiftly, followed immediately by Lord Peacock and Lady Bluebird. Hyla and Saddleback both arrived moments later, one after the other, having also heard the call and clearly understanding its urgent nature. Those on board the Cobalt Cloud all joined with Tryxie on its bow, who'd brought them side by side with the ship of their allies.

Prince Heron stood triumphantly in the circular opening of the window frame and gazed intently at the incoming forces, specifically Captain Cardinal. The prince looked much different than the crimson captain had seen him in Jack Diamond's dream. Fashioned into a war machine, not a part of him had the appearance of being organic anymore. Unfailingly noticeable was a golden crown upon his head, which glistened in the red morning sun. The drawbridge lowered as Heron descended to his prey. Bishop and Kestrel held the dishonored and beaten king up in front of his domineering son.

"What—are you doing?" King Eagle screeched, coughing up blood, the ground beneath him cast even redder.

"What I have to," Heron scolded.

"You're—cough—alive," the king said bitterly, weeping. "We—cough—I—cough—thought you were—cough—dead."

Heron retorted, "I did die, father, and it's your fault."

The king was shocked and confused, demanding, "What—cough—my son, did you—cough?"

"Your son is dead. Prince Heron is dead. I am King Heron now."

"I don't—cough—understand," King Eagle replied as he painfully surveyed his augmented progeny's cybernetic physique. "As my son—cough, you—cough—were a prince, the—cough—prince. You were a king!" Choking up another mass of blood, his life was depleting rapidly.

Laughing in derision, Heron refuted, "No I wasn't. Come on, father, you read the prophecy. You get a new son, remember? 'An heir born not unto him shall inherit the king's throne,' it says."

"I—cough, cough—mourn my son—cough. You—cough, cough, cough—defile his memory." Summoning everything he had left, he looked Heron dead in the eye and reprimanded him. "My son—cough—looked to the day with pride—cough—when he would serve Captain Cardinal—cough, cough—whose authority is higher even than mine, and whose kingdom is far greate—"

Instead of blood choking him this time, Heron's cold brutal grip of death around his neck cut him off, and Bishop and Kestrel consequently released their hold.

"It doesn't matter," Heron dismissed, "I operate under my own authority now. I am King Heron, and I will destroy you and Captain Cardinal. Cloud Castle and Volar are mine." Spitefully, he crushed the windpipe of his broken predecessor and callously dropped him to crumple on the scattered jagged rosy fragments beneath him.

As he turned, Razorbill met him from inside the castle. He pulled out a scrolled parchment and untied it. Kneeling down, he picked up one of King Eagle's own white crown feathers and dipped the quill in the spilled blood of his father. After writing a brief declaration on the scroll, the self-appointed king rolled it back up and handed it to Razorbill, ordering his new subordinate, "Go, and take this to Captain Cardinal."

Razorbill received the scroll and zoomed undaunted toward the Crimson Crest, with Bishop and Kestrel tailing him closely. The panoply of heroes prepared for the trio's quickly-impending arrival with weapons ready. As the three drew near, Captain Cardinal raised his hand to hold off the attack. He had a feeling the tables were about to turn.

Razorbill touched down presumptuously, along with the two former lords, on the crimson deck and stood face to face with the prophesied hero. Heron's arrogant representative held up the scroll in front of Captain Cardinal's emboldened visage and let it roll out. Bloody letters spelled out the statement that their previously surreptitious adversary had made moments ago to the one he had devastatingly ripped the title from:

I AM KING HERON.

Chapter XIX – Resurrection

The reaction of Captain Cardinal and his comrades wasn't at all in line with the intention of intimidation. Momentarily, the perplexed Razorbill, along with his accomplices, noticed the claw-like slash marks that had inexplicably appeared through the letters, and their bravado quickly died. Captain Cardinal, along with those who saw the sign, began to chortle with excitement. Razorbill looked back just in time to see Heron being grabbed by furry claws through a swirling mass of color that was like a much smaller Rainbow Veil. For once, he had no idea what to do.

"Phoenix Prime is with us," Captain Cardinal declared.

Sounds of victory came from all those aboard both ships.

"Razorbill," Captain Cardinal said to him, "it seems no matter who you align yourself with, you lose. I'm surprised Peregrine has let you get this far."

Razorbill was painfully aware of his utter defeat, and his anger and disappointment shifted to dread when he heard the familiar voice.

"You have a funny way of knowing when I'm about to show up," Peregrine said, suddenly appearing in the air next to the Crimson Crest.

"Peregrine," the captain acknowledged, surprised to see him.

Acting in fear, Bishop and Kestrel pointed their

new weapons at Peregrine and tried to torch him, but the latter vaulted upward and did a somersault in between the two, slicing them off. Fortunately, only a small fireball combusted behind him, sending a cascade of flaming oil away from the ship. Subsequently, he removed Razorbill's new hand replacement for good measure, and for spite.

"Bishop and Kestrel," Peregrine acknowledged. "Like two sides of the same coin. Nice to see you together, but it looks like you both also chose poorly. What are you going to do now?"

They looked at each other and shrugged.

"What are you going to do now, Peregrine?" Captain Cardinal asked him intently.

"I came here for Razorbill," Peregrine confirmed, pointing his bounty's own sickle at him.

"Be good," the captain warned Razorbill, who was getting riled.

Staying his anger through a clenched beak, Razorbill relented, "Fine, you win," and he handed the captain the scroll.

Bishop and Kestrel, having abandoned any malicious intent themselves, were ready to see what would happen next. Checking for further contention from Peregrine, the captain pointed at Razorbill with a curious expression to see what he would do.

"Relax, Captain, Razorbill is no good to anyone dead," Peregrine assured him. "Besides, you have your own dead to look after," he said grimly, glancing at Volar.

Razorbill was relieved but uncertain as to his fate.

Captain Cardinal appealed to Peregrine, saying, "Peregrine, you know the truth about me now. Whatever you plan to do with Razorbill, let it wait. Phoenix Prime is about to do something miraculous, and you're not going to want to miss this."

"What is that, Captain?"

"We must go on to Volar."

"I'll be waiting," Peregrine said, and he disappeared.

Without missing a beat, Captain Cardinal turned and cried to Captain Blue Jay, "Follow me, Captain."

"Understood, Captain," came the reply.

Within minutes, they arrived on Volar, and they disembarked quickly. When the entire team and their visitors had gathered together, they waited for Captain Cardinal to speak. Peregrine perched on a branch close to Sir Albatross, curious himself about where the captain was going.

"Everyone, wait here," he instructed, and he flew to the body of the beloved fallen king.

Most of them thought he was simply going to retrieve the body of King Eagle for burial, but there was the allusion to something unexpected. Peregrine was still bitter about the king, however, and because his death now also brought accusation, he resisted looking directly at the corpse.

Sensing this, Sir Albatross looked up at him and said kindly, "Peregrine, I'm relieved I don't have to fight you today. I'm glad you're here, my friend."

"You won't have to again, unless you want to," Peregrine teased.

"Challenge accepted," Albatross returned, glad to have his friend back.

They clasped forearms, but their attention was quickly diverted back to Captain Cardinal.

Kneeling next to the king's body, the captain was beginning to pray in his signature unknown language, and the atmosphere rapidly charged around him. After several moments, his eyes suddenly opened, ablaze. He stood, drawing the Ruby Edge, and the air around its blade immediately began to ignite. Looking up, he said loudly and reverently, "Thank you, Phoenix Prime. We give you the honor, the glory, and the praise for what you are about to do. I thank you that these here are all witnesses to your awesome power. Be glorified in me, and me in you. Amen."

"Amen," several of them echoed.

He lowered the flaming edge of his legendary sword to King Eagle's chest, setting the carcass on fire. No one made a protest, but almost everyone watched with anticipation. Razorbill still really had no idea what was going on. As the body burned, Captain Cardinal gave thanks again. He made his way toward the group, and no one dared to speak. He turned back around and waited with them until the fire finished burning. The ashy heap left behind was not grey, but almost looked like flecks of gold. "Arise, King Golden Eagle," he cried. "Return from the ashes."

The ash began to tremble and fall away as a radiant form began to appear. A pair of glistening wings sprang out, sending clouds of glittering ash and cinder into the air, creating a spectacular display. The reborn king cried out, arching up. The silence had been broken, and there was much excitement.

"Are you seeing this?" Lord Peacock asked Lady Bluebird.

"I can't believe it," she cried. "You know what this means?"

"I do," he replied. He held her and licked her beak, which was the Avian way of kissing.

Peregrine had seen more than anyone else what Captain Cardinal brought to the table, but neither he nor Sir Albatross could believe the phenomenon. "This is crazy," he said.

"This is… Captain Cardinal," is all Albatross had for a reply.

The king stood, ruffling his feathers and flapping his wings, creating another golden cascade as he shook off the remaining dust.

"King Golden Eagle," Captain Cardinal said, addressing him.

"Captain Cardinal," he replied. "Thank you for bringing me back."

"Thank Phoenix Prime."

"Yes, thank Phoenix Prime."

"How do you feel, Your Majesty?"

"I feel marvelous, Captain. There is much you and I can now speak of together that was only on the edges of my ability to grasp before. My body feels lighter and faster than it ever was, and this plumage is glorious."

"Yes, Your Majesty, it truly is magnificent," came a voice he had longed to hear.

"Barbary, my queen," he uttered with excitement, opening his arms to receive her tender embrace. "Seeing you now, I could die again happy."

The spectators were filled with the utmost joy at this royal reunion.

After savoring the moment for as long as possible, the king inquired, "What has become of our son?"

"Heron has been taken," Captain Cardinal answered.

"Taken?"

"Through a portal. He was kidnapped by an Animystian with furry claws," the captain elaborated. Holding up the scroll given to him by Razorbill, he continued, "This was supposed to be a threat from your son, but when it was opened for my eyes, it had claw marks slashed through it. We assumed they belonged to the Grey Fox, since it happened so quickly and mysteriously, and the Grey Fox helped us before."

"Let me see it, Captain."

"Of course, Your Majesty." The captain handed him the scroll.

Opening and observing it, King Golden Eagle stated, "This looks like the Leonin."

"I know who their contact here is," Peregrine said, stepping in to join the conversation at the behest of Sir Albatross. Razorbill found himself there with them.

The king offered his hand, saying, "Peregrine, no, Lord Peregrine, welcome home."

"Welcome back," Peregrine quipped, accepting it.

"I see you've had some work done yourself," the king jested, indicating Peregrine's wings.

"We've got a lot to catch up on."

"Indeed, we have."

"Are we going after Heron?" Sir Albatross inquired. The king and queen looked at each other.

"He's still our son, King Golden Eagle said.

"Yes," Queen Barbary affirmed.

"Razorbill," he addressed compassionately, "it looks like you've had it rough. Have you joined us now?"

"I think I'm done joining," he replied. "Maybe it's time to go it alone.

"If you stay with us here, it will be different for you. You won't have to scheme for power and prestige. There will be honor and peace for you."

Razorbill wasn't ready to make that commitment, but he did offer, "King Golden Eagle, I will help you find your son. We'll see what happens after that."

"Fair enough, thank you, Razorbill."

"He'll come with me to talk to our contact," Peregrine suggested.

"Well, he's really everyone's contact, if you ask me," Captain Blue Jay said facetiously, joining the company and conversation. "Tryxie and I know where they're going."

"That's right, we do," she confirmed.

The king said, "Very well, Captain Blue Jay," then commanded him, "Take Tryxie, Peregrine, and Razorbill. Send word for a rendezvous when you are ready."

"As you wish, Your Majesty."

"Captain Cardinal?"

"Yes, King Golden Eagle?"

"Are you ready?"

"I was born ready."

"Indeed, you were, Captain Cardinal. Indeed, you were. Now, get your team assembled. I'll send word to King Leo. We're going to the Eastern Realm."

—THE END—